"Do you ever ask you **went wrong, Ulfric?"** **deliberately. Reckless** **curdled within your soul to make you like this?"**

He felt that edgy, deliciously cruel twist in the corner of his mouth. He watched as her eyes widened and knew she saw it for what it was. A warning she did not intend to heed.

Too easily could he read the foolhardy glitter in her gaze. And he knew as well as she did that she did this willfully.

He knew what she wanted.

Because he knew, as she did, that when their particular fire rose so high between them, they both craved the burn of it. That impossible burn, that unforgettable release.

They were two halves of the same whole. Well did he know it. But never more than at moments like this.

Author Note

One of the things I love most about historicals is the intersection of the needy human heart and the ability of women, specifically, to meet the challenge of their times. Few things make me happier than reading through a dense bit of research and then reminding myself that people are ever and always will be people. It's often my way into a scene and into the hearts of my hero and heroine no matter what might be going on around them.

But it's the particular fortitude of women, so often the unsung heroes of their own stories, that I love the most in these books (and in life!). *The Viking's Runaway Concubine* is set during the Viking Age, when an Irish girl living through various wars in Dublin could look forward to a very brief life by our standards. As I researched the years that interested me, I repeatedly encountered sentences in the accounts that read something like, *And, of course, the Viking's primary export was slaves.* Indeed, in Iceland today, more than 60 percent of Icelandic women have Irish ancestry, directly because of that slave trade. Some scholars believe that the Viking Age itself was less about land and more about women.

But who were those women?

What did they feel, think, fear?

Who did they love—and how did they make the best of what befell them?

This book is a take on what might have happened when history and the human heart collide. I hope you love it!

CAITLIN CREWS

The Viking's
Runaway Concubine

HARLEQUIN

HISTORICAL

HARLEQUIN®
HISTORICAL™

ISBN-13: 978-1-335-72333-8

The Viking's Runaway Concubine

Copyright © 2022 by Caitlin Crews

For questions and comments about the quality of this book,
please contact us at CustomerService@Harlequin.com.

Harlequin Enterprises ULC
22 Adelaide St. West, 41st Floor
Toronto, Ontario M5H 4E3, Canada
www.Harlequin.com

Printed in U.S.A.

Recycling programs
for this product may
not exist in your area.

USA TODAY bestselling and RITA® Award–nominated author **Caitlin Crews** loves writing romance. She teaches her favorite romance novels in creative-writing classes at places like UCLA Extension's prestigious Writers' Program, where she finally gets to utilize the MA and PhD in English literature she received from the University of York in England. She currently lives in the Pacific Northwest with her very own hero and too many pets. Visit her at caitlincrews.com.

Books by Caitlin Crews

Harlequin Historical

Kidnapped by the Viking
The Viking's Runaway Concubine

Look out for more books from Caitlin Crews coming soon.

Visit the Author Profile page
at Harlequin.com.

Chapter One

Jorvik, June 919 AD

The dream woke her in a rush of red heat and shame, his name on her lips like a terrible curse.

Or, worse yet, a prayer. Soft and full of flame, as her body yet shook with a need she only pretended she'd left behind her. While the sun shined, she pretended as best she could—and yet at night, the truth stalked her and these dreams woke her as they ended the way she always had, shaking apart in his hands.

Eithne knew better than to move upon waking. She knew better than to call such attention to herself. She woke too fast yet kept herself still, her eyes screwed shut, as she fought to contain the urge within her to scream, to flail, to make those noises she had always swallowed down, no matter how difficult. She told herself she meant to push the dream away. To push *him* away as she should have done then.

But she had learned her lessons too well. The dream

still held her fast, but with every breath, she saw a little further past it. Soon enough, she remembered herself. She was no longer trapped in his furs, subject to his pagan wickedness. She had escaped him. She had changed her fate. She shared this pallet with Osthryth, the old Mercian woman who was yet her salvation.

Salvation snored this early morn, a rough music that slowly penetrated the wild red haze within Eithne. Slowly, slowly, it brought her, if not peace—for what was peace in this damaged world of might and men, pitiless and wretched from one sea to the next—then quiet within Eithne, where before there was naught but that infernal noise, that impossible *ache*.

Osthryth's snores meant safety.

After some more moments passed, her blood high, she allowed herself to believe it.

Eithne opened her eyes slowly, taking in the dim outlines of this crowded dwelling on the outskirts of busy Jorvik. She could smell the smoke from the central fire and the sour rushes on the floor, for Osthryth's kinswoman was a bitter creature who had no pride in her home, rude and cramped though it was.

Not like Eithne. Her mother had raised her to keep whatever dwelling she found herself in clean and neat. She had sung while she worked, but that life was long gone now. Her girlhood was as much a dream to her now as *he* was, and she would have much rather dreamed of those days than of him.

But well did Eithne know that her mother was long

dead. And Dublin was across the sea from these hostile lands. She had no hope that she would see it again this life.

She told herself it mattered not. There was nothing there save misery.

The red tendrils of the dream seemed to tighten around her again then, and she did her best to push them away. She sat up, taking care to move as if her bones creaked and ached, the way Osthryth's did. That was the first thing Osthryth had taught her when she'd encountered the old woman in the woods. Eithne had been running for days by then, hungry and terrified, certain that at any moment she would be caught and killed.

You are a fair sight too pretty to kill, I fear, the old woman had rasped when Eithne had told her what she'd done. Her gaze had been as steady as it was something like sorry. As if she knew exactly what a curse it was to have a pretty face in a world where men ravaged lands for what treasures they could find. Then took them at will. *They will use you first and make you wish you'd cut your own throat.*

It wasn't that Eithne hadn't thought of doing exactly that. She'd waited near a full year for him to trust her enough that he might leave his weapons where she could reach them. And even on that fateful night when he'd finally done it, when she'd finally picked up that dagger of his and gripped it in her hands, for a giddy, reckless moment she hadn't known if she planned to cut him or her.

I confess I might indeed wish such a sinful thing, she

had told the old woman. *But there are yet men needing killing.*

They'd been huddling around a fire in the lonely woods, where Osthryth had been scavenging for roots and mushrooms and other ingredients for the salves and poultices she made that she would not teach Eithne for months yet. And Eithne had half expected the old woman to condemn her then, for talking too easily of mortal sins like killing, but Osthryth had only laughed. More rueful than amused.

There always are, child, she had said. *More all the time in this dark age.*

The first thing she'd done was teach Eithne how to alter her appearance. How to rub her black hair with ash, until it looked as gray as Osthryth's. What nuts to chew to make her teeth look brown and stained. How to hold herself so that she looked three times her age, and could be of no possible interest to men and their lusts. Over time, Eithne had added a hump on her back so that she looked stooped and gnarled.

It was a freedom she would never take for granted again.

In the woods, alone, she walked as she liked. Upright, her feet steady on this cold, foreign soil she'd been brought to against her will. In the woods, she drank in every bit of precious, rare light she could find in that first frigid Northumbrian winter. It was only when she and Osthryth went down into the scattered villages that she practiced her shuffle, her uneven gait.

Better to make them uneasy, not scare them outright, Osthryth had cackled after Eithne's initial attempt at the first village they'd come to, a day's walk from the woods where Osthryth had found her. *'Tis too easy to call a healer woman a witch when the winter grows too dark.*

But winter had passed. The bright spring had come, then the easy days of summer. Eithne was a good student, and by the time winter came again she had picked up the old woman's knowledge as if she'd been thirsting for it all her life. Then, too, she liked to think she had brought her own secrets with her, gleaned in her girlhood from her grandmother, her mother. All the women she'd lost.

As if she honored them thus.

And she would always dream of crossing the cold sea once more and finding her way back to what was left of the Dublin she'd known, in those years when she'd grown up so heedless of the fate awaiting her. When she'd imagined that her people had rid themselves of the Northmen scourge forever. For she had been but little when the Irish Kings had thrown them out, and well did she recall the stories the men told of that great victory.

It was tempting to wonder what might have happened if her father had lived. If he and her mother had not succumbed to the illness that had swept through their home that terrible winter, taking not only her parents but the rest of her brothers and sisters besides, save Feargal.

In the dark of that little dwelling in Jorvik, Eithne

lay on her pallet and thought of her brother Feargal, feeling all that leftover wild red within her turn into a blade, sharp and deadly.

For I will cross that sea again if I must swim it like a fish, she promised herself, as she always did. *And if he yet lives, I will greet my brother as he deserves.*

The purity of her hatred was cleansing. It almost felt like bathing herself the way she longed to do. She missed the clear streams in the forests, where she could immerse her whole body and let the water wash these last years away while Osthryth muttered prayers for deliverance from such pagan pursuits and kept the fire going.

But to bathe like that in a place like this would reveal her, even if she dared brave the crowded riverbanks here. It was no more available to her than a swift boat across the Irish Sea to take her back home, still clutching the dagger she'd taken when she'd escaped her captor and cut him as she went.

Eithne would have to settle for the bright, cold fire of her hatred instead.

Truly, it was her closest friend, so close did she carry it.

She sat with it there in the dark a while longer, nursing it. All around, Osthryth's kinsfolk slept crowded in around the open hearth. There had been no meat for the stew these last nights, though privately, Eithne suspected that Osthryth's kinswoman did not wish to waste what meat she might have on two old, worthless women. And in that, Eithne could not rightly blame her. For the poor woman had six children to feed and a man who came home with no fish, reeking of ale. These were cramped conditions and hard times, even in Jorvik, which so many villagers Eithne had met over her travels this last year had spoken of with awe.

For surely Jorvik must be a sacred place indeed, one villager had told her with great confidence, far to the north. *Else why should so many fight to claim it for so long?*

Eithne had nodded sagely when what she'd truly wished to do was lecture the man on river access and Northmen fleets, kings and their blood-soaked wars. But well had she learned that no man, even an aged farmer in fields far away from the sound of any battle, wished to hear a woman's opinions. Particularly if said opinions were both correct and contrary to his own.

Never let it be said I cannot learn, she thought dryly.

Eithne crept from her pallet, drawing her ragged clothes around her as she moved. She knew the outer cloak was most important, tattered and torn as it looked, telling any who gazed upon her that she was little more than a crone. Withered and beneath notice. She picked her way across the small hut, careful not to look too nimble. Though she thought she was the only soul awake, there was no way to be sure and there was no point in risking discovery. She and Osthryth were to spend but one more day here selling their wares, offering healing and hope in equal measure to the women who sought them out, before moving on. Far away from this treacherous place and back into the safety of the dark Northumbrian woods.

Eithne made it across the crowded floor, then eased her way out the door, slipping out into the last gasp of night. As she had done every night they had been here, when the dreams tortured her awake and she could no longer bear to lie still. She closed the door behind her, then huddled against it. Even in the dark, this Jorvik was a grimy, gritty place. There were people everywhere, strange men in odd costumes speaking languages Eithne could not fathom. Men slept outside, for they had no dwellings of their own and partook too much of ale. Their snores were rougher than Osthryth's, and yet gave her no sense of well-being. The smell of livestock and refuse rose thick in the air, and even before dawn, when it seemed only she stirred, Eithne could sense the danger here.

It was like its own smoke in the air. Like a hand at her throat. And she knew she would not truly be easy until she and Osthryth left this place today, making their slow and steady way back out into the wild forests, where there was quiet. Fewer eyes to look upon them. Woods to swallow them whole and allow them to walk and talk as they pleased, with no worry that they might be watched.

The wild forests, where *he* was not.

Eithne swallowed hard, for if there were a hand at her throat, she knew well it was his.

She reached her hand into the deep pockets of her cloak and felt the reassuring weight of his dagger, strapped to her hip. She kept to the shadows outside the small dwelling, not wishing to draw any attention to herself as she stood, hunched over like a crone, and let herself feel all the things she dared not show in the light of day.

It had been like this since they had arrived here. It was as if she could feel him, as surely as if she looked upon him with her own eyes again. That hard face, etched in bold lines that led straight to his mouth like stone. His dark blond hair in thick braids, his midnight gaze knowing and implacable.

She shivered, though the summer morning was not cold.

It would be better when they quit this place.

For it had been a long year since she'd cut him with his own dagger and fled. More than a year. Eithne had hoped that he might fall in battle, like so many men did, but she knew too well he had not. She would have heard of it if he had—whenever great warriors fell, the songs soon followed. Like many, she had hoped that the Lady of the Mercians, a queen in this land of too many warring kings, might turn back these Northmen at last. For they were the very same clan the Irish Kings had ejected from Dublin when Eithne was a babe.

They had retaken Dublin—and *he* had taken her. Over the sea and into Northumbria to fight at Corbridge, then on to Jorvik, where it was thought they might finally be beaten off for good—but the Lady had fallen last summer. Soon after, Jorvik had been claimed by Ragnall, a kinsman of Sitric, who even now ruled her beloved Dublin.

Dublin, where her brother had sold her without a second thought to gain favor and save his own skin—but she could not think of Feargal. Not where others might look upon her face and see her hatred bloom unchecked.

This was Jorvik, where Ragnall had now ruled for the whole of a long year. There was no safety here. For wherever Ragnall was, Eithne knew, so, too, was *he*.

And only here, in the rancid dark of the summer morning, where Eithne had the freedom she had claimed for herself by spilling his blood—the only real currency in these days of war and sorrow—she allowed herself to think his name.

Ulfric.

A mighty warrior, his name spoken in honor and sung in mead halls, though Eithne cared nothing for men's dark deeds. Ulfric, feared wherever he stood, beloved by Ragnall, and for too long, her master.

Out here in what was left of the dark, Eithne closed her eyes tight and did not try to hide the deep shiver that rolled through her, a betraying red heat made of equal parts shame and fury that she knew anyone watching would mistake for the ravages of age.

When what it was, in truth, was an ache deep inside, a longing, that she'd come to think akin to the weakness some men had for their ale.

He had made her a drunkard. In her dreams, she still drank deep.

She would kill him for that, had she only the opportunity. With his own blade or die trying.

And she stood there as the day broke over this accursed place where the Ouse and the Foss met, as close to him as she had been in over a year. As close to him as she intended to be for the remainder of her life. Or his, which she hoped would be brutally short, for there were even now whispers of Edward of Wessex, who had already claimed Mercia. There were always worries about the bloodthirsty Danes and the brutal Scots. They would rise, as they always did, one after the next. Men claimed they wanted only land, but little did they tend to what they had whenever there were blades to swing or songs to sing of brave deeds in battle.

Ulfric would serve his King forever. And Ragnall had set up his court here in Jorvik, for with her own eyes she had seen his coin in the marketplace and heard tales of him and his men. It was risky to be here, that was certain, though it were unlikely that any Northmen would seek out the services of two old crones and the salves and ointments they peddled to the women who had need of them.

Ulfric would serve his King, and kings had a tendency to die horribly, and maybe someday these lands would be free of them both. Maybe then these dreams would leave Eithne in peace, and she would think no more of that year she had served him.

That year he had taken her body and bruised her soul, making her little more than a wicked flame who danced at his bidding.

She felt the dagger in her hand, and no, she would not forgive that, either.

Eithne knew he slept here, somewhere in this dirty gathering place of too many people, too many grim-eyed warriors and fishermen, slavers and tradesmen from afar. She knew he slept here and she hoped only that he woke remembering his own steel at his throat, the murder in her green eyes, and was uneasy.

Every morn had she wished thus, and tomorrow she and Osthryth would be gone.

She intended to think of him no more.

Trade was brisk that day.

For word had got about that the old, wizened healer women were leaving, so those who had taken their time in coming to them tarried no longer. Osthryth counseled two heavily pregnant women on how best to prepare for their coming births. Eithne quietly prepared a selection of herbs for a young girl who came with her mother, speaking brightly of her coming wedding.

"So much does her husband desire her that he is half-mad with it," said the girl's mother, and though her laugh was merry on the breeze, her eyes were cool on Eithne's. "It would be a pity if he were to think others had been where he has decreed only he may go, would it not?" She laughed again, and her gaze turned to her daughter. "These men and their conquests, forever in search of untouched lands. They will be the death of us all."

"It is ever so," Eithne agreed. She handed the bundle of herbs to the girl. "But there is nothing to fear. When he claims you, you need only tuck this where you bleed each moon and he will imagine only he has ever done so."

The girl's eyes were wide and hopeful, telling Eithne more than she needed to know about the future that awaited her. A man's temper, a man's fists. A man who strutted about believing himself king of his own dwelling, at the least, while his woman must forever bend and twine herself around him, his happiness her own health.

If there were men in these cursed lands who did not behave thus, Eithne had never heard tell of them.

"Thank you," the girl's mother said quietly, pressing a coin into Eithne's hand—a far greater payment than she would have requested. "It is best to begin a marriage with all the advantages, I think. For time and the gods will do as they will, no matter what."

Eithne did not blaspheme aloud in public, though she found herself wondering which was the worst. Time and the gods, as the woman said?

Or these men who battered the world into their image, so concerned with glory that they left naught but ruin behind?

She was happy, after the woman and the girl left her, to pack up their remaining wares. She was already breathing easier at the prospect of leaving this eve, walking until dark. She did not like these crowded places. She could not. Too well did she remember how it had been in Dublin after the Northmen came. The crowds of people thrown from their homes. The dead. The pyres. The misery.

The slave auction.

She felt something cold skate its way down her back, and found herself glancing around, as if deadly eyes were upon her. But she saw only the sprawl of Jorvik.

It was likely no more than memories. Yet another reason to put this place behind her.

Last summer they had not come here, fearing unrest in the wake of the Lady of Mercia's death. But there had been no question but to come this summer. The more they sold, the better the winter. That was the way of it. And there were always more sales to be had in a place with more people. Still, as practical as she knew it was to come to this grimy city, Eithne thought it would take some time to get the stain of it off her.

As if she would need, once more, to shift his weight from her body. As if he still sprawled there, all of that heat and muscle, battle-ready and bold, pressing her down into his furs—

Eithne blew out a ragged breath as she walked, headed back to Osthryth's kinswoman's hut, slipping between the dwellings crowded in together as she went. They would collect their few possessions, bid their farewells.

She was thinking how good it would feel to put Jorvik at her back at last—

And in the next moment, everything was spinning.

Then she was slammed up, hard, against the nearest wooden wall.

Her hands rose in a fake surrender, for well did she know that a bit of cringing went a long way. For it was ever thus that predators were drawn to weakness. It was why she hid the better part of the coin she'd made on her person, but kept a more accessible purse with only a few bits at the ready.

But when she lifted her gaze, she froze.

Her nightmare reared before her, only this was no red dream.

He was *here*.

She could feel the fury come off him in waves. As if it was smoke and flame. As if he was.

One hand braced against the wall beside her, his other hand fast at her throat. Not choking her. She only wished he would choke her, for then it would be over.

Instead, he merely held her in that way he had held her so many times before.

He stood above her, blocking out the sun, his shoulders wider than she recalled. His cloak finer. His face drawn crueler—with the scar she'd left him across one cheek.

And to her horror she felt a little curl of wicked sensation wind around and around within her, shaming her anew.

"Eithne, my little slave," Ulfric growled at her, his dark eyes afire. "You have made yet another terrible mistake."

Chapter Two

Ulfric had known he would find her again.

He had known it, even in those first moments when the extent of her betrayal became clear. He had believed it, even though the days did pass, winter turned to summer and came back around again. He had taken to rubbing his fingers over the scar she'd left him, to remind him. To make it a certainty that she was never far from his thoughts.

For she never was, in all this time. And he had been certain they would meet again.

Now he stared down at Eithne's face, etched forever in his head whether he wished it or no, and the flashing green eyes that had given her away. She was otherwise unrecognizable. From a distance she looked like the crone she pretended she was, gnarled of limb and matted hair. Even as he held her fast against the wall of the dwelling they stood beside, she was lopsided. He could see that what looked like an old woman's hump on her back must be some kind of fabric, wadded up to give the impression of age and infirmity from afar.

That she dared—that she *dared*—was a pounding drum within him.

To leave him. To hide from him. To imagine she could present herself in this disguise and yet evade him.

And if he was more relieved than he wished to be— that she yet lived, that she was hale and hearty enough to bother disguising herself, that she had not died soon after running from his tent—he kept that locked away. Because this was about property, he told himself.

This could only be about the fact she had taken *his property* from him. He should have cared only that he had claimed her once again—not about her condition.

Not as if she mattered more to him than she should.

"Are you not pleased to see me?" he demanded, his voice low and his fury simmering within him, coming out in a dangerous growl when he thought it were a likelihood that his temper alone could raze Jorvik to the ground. If he gave in to it, what could stand? "Have you forgotten how to greet your master?"

He stroked the side of her throat almost absently. Almost as if his fingers moved of their own accord. She had spread the same filth that stained her face down that slender column, but he could feel the truth beneath his palm. He could feel her youth, her warmth, her softness. He felt the wildfire of that connection, as he had ever done.

He could feel *her*. Eithne.

Mine, a voice in him whispered, like a single bell rung deep.

Everything in him, his battle-honed fury, his driving need to find what was his and show her his displeasure… shifted.

And he accepted what some part of him must have known all along. That his fury at Eithne's treachery only made his lust for her all the greater.

For he had always known that, even more than most men, he found his satisfaction in the darker places. A woman's usual surrender pleased him, but far deeper was his pleasure in pushing the boundaries of that surrender. He had indulged himself in the women who flocked to him, eyes soft and bright when tales of his bravery were told in the night—and he had learned how to tailor his needs to make certain of their pleasure, always yearning for his own.

Always hoping that one day, he might find the full pleasure he sought.

And no woman had ever pleased him so well as this one.

He could feel her pulse, a mad clattering in her neck. He could feel it when she swallowed, fear and apprehension and something more, something that matched the howling hunger in him. For he knew her too well, this woman who had haunted him for almost as long as she'd lain with him. He knew her body better than he knew his own. It held no secrets from him, not the way she had. She was his own private ghost.

"I can see you thinking." He put his face close to hers, his mouth near her ear, witness then to the fine tremor running through her that she tried to conceal. "Drawing up your little plots again. Trying to find a way to hide. Will you pretend you cannot speak this time? How much did that cost you, I wonder? It was one thing not to use words when your silence was a weapon, but you and I both know it must have torn you apart not to cry out your pleasure in my furs." He laughed a little when she pressed her lips together, much as if she planned to defy him anew. "Do as you please, Eithne. But I have already heard your voice, speaking as if you were never mute to begin with, right here in the market square."

She didn't fight him, but not because she didn't wish it with every part of her. He could see from her gaze alone that she wished him naught but violent ends.

It only made his cock heavier, for he had always liked her spirit. The challenge of her, mixed in with the particular sweetness of her surrender.

He also liked that she obviously remembered all too well how easily he had mastered her.

As he would again.

Her chest heaved as if she were running, though he kept her pinned to the wall and yes, she remembered. He could feel the heat in her flesh, those memories made real.

"You are a devil," she said, spitting the words at him, each one its own blade.

Yet Ulfric only laughed, because she was in his hands once again.

And finally, finally, she deigned to speak to him.

He didn't like to think how many times he had wished she might while he'd had her in his furs, mutinous until he had coaxed her into sighs and sobs, and that sweet honey between her legs. Even now, he suspected that if he reached down between them and found his way beneath her tattered clothes, he would find her already damp and ready for him.

For she always was, and no matter that she might hate him.

"A devil I may be," he agreed, his mouth so close to her. It would have been on her already, were she less dirty. "And so you have marked me. If only so that all can see your passion drawn like runes into my flesh."

Eithne liked that very little indeed. She stiffened against his words, but the heat in her flesh only deepened.

As did the ways he wanted her. The ways he had dreamed of having her once more.

No longer were they dreams. For she was once again in his hands, and he would not make the same mistake twice. He would not trust her again.

"I would think a great warrior would know the difference between passion and simple bloodlust," she threw at him, and he found himself moving closer to her so he could wedge his body against hers, holding her fast in more ways than one.

Because there was no possible claim he could put upon this woman that was enough.

Ulfric had spent these long months without her coming to terms with that. He did not simply wish to collect his property, as any man would. As he had at last. But more, he wanted to mark her. Own her in such a way that she could never again stray a single step from his side without the whole world noting that she had done so. Without it being perfectly clear where she belonged.

"It is not blood you lust for, little slave." He inspected her hair, holding up a lank strand and rolling it between his fingers. Ash, he discovered. Not dirt. A costume like the rest. "Though we may yet spill some blood, you and I. The gods saw fit to throw you in my path once more, and you must know well that they will need a reckoning. Or you would not have tried to conceal your true face, would you?"

She shoved at him then, and he liked it. Her shoves were nothing to him but proof that he was as far beneath her skin as she was under his, like an itch he could never scratch enough for any relief. She might as well shove a mountain. He only grunted some little bit. Then he lifted her hands, ending their fruitless attempts to dislodge him—and removing the temptation to reach for one of his weapons—while taking care to look at one side, then the other. Not at the dirt that covered her, but their condition.

"Your hands," he grunted. "You have hardened them."

Ulfric liked a woman with soft hands, and he had kept her as he liked her—because he could. Many men used their concubines for labor beyond the work they did on their backs, but he had not required that of Eithne. That she tend to him, yes. But he had not accorded her the most unpleasant tasks, because it had never been his wish to crush her.

But to indulge in her.

And there was part of him that disliked the state of her now. That wondered if this was his failing, that she had fallen so. For it were a certainty that it was a master's duty to protect his slave and keep her from harm, and he had not done so, in the end. He would need to think on that. But not now.

For though there was a part of him that might have raged at the rough places he could feel on her fingers for that was not his preference, there was another part of him that could think only of how her newly roughened hands might feel against his cock.

As she performed one of the tasks he liked best.

Eithne tried to tug the hand he held out of his grasp and failed. "I use my hands to work, as we all must do if we are not beloved by kings and showered in gold for bloody deeds. I use them for their God-given purpose. Not the idle sins you bathe in daily."

"Better to bathe than be mistaken for the trash in the street," he replied, not the least offended by her talk of sin and idleness. For one, there was no truth in such claims. And for another, his gods did not traffic in the scandalized morality these Christians loved so well.

His gods sang songs of flesh, of blood. They demanded rituals, not prayers. Sacrifice and pain, not bloodless masses and the pious rantings of corrupt priests.

Eithne had not told him of her beliefs before. She had not used her voice before at all, yet still, he had known well enough that she found his ways an affront.

Until she did not, that was.

"You think that an insult," she was gritting out, her green eyes flashing. "But I would die happy tomorrow if you mistook me for trash in this street. I wish you would."

"Have you led a blameless life, then?" he asked her, almost as if it were an afterthought. "Your God-given purpose...that you earned at the point of a blade, drawing blood like a pagan?"

She shuddered at that, and Ulfric felt it shake through him. And this was not a dream. He would not wake in his usual fever in his furs, without her. Missing her in ways he did not like to admit. This slave girl who he had shared too much of himself with, believing she could not whisper his secrets to another. Believing she would not leave him if she could.

He had found her—that was what mattered. He shook off the odd sensation of betrayal that had stalked him these long months, that she had done this to him.

Not the scar on his face, for where was he not scarred? He wore the marks on his body proudly.

But that she had made a mockery of the tenderness he had felt only and ever for her.

Ulfric did not intend to make that mistake again. What did he care what condition she was in? She was his. He would make her what he wished her to be once again.

In truth, he would enjoy it.

"All I wish is to be left alone," she told him then, her voice more urgent. Her expression was as close to imploring as he had seen yet, and he felt another shift in him. For too well did he like it when she begged, and now he could hear the words. That notion moved in him like strong ale, though it was not his head that throbbed. "Can you not simply let me go?"

Ulfric stood back then, though he kept that hand at her throat.

Because it pleased him to hold her thus, as it ever had.

And his arm was long enough that he could study the rest of her. This disguise she must have spent some time perfecting. Who would look twice at this woman? Too old, too brittle. A rattle of bones wearing a few rags, nothing more.

He found that despite the dark fury that did beat in him still, he admired it.

"Please, Ulfric," she said, so softly.

So prettily.

And it was better than all the times he had dreamed he might hear her say his name. That he might hear her beg him for mercy.

It was so much better that he laughed for the sheer joy of it. He threw back his head and let the sound boom out of him, far rustier than he remembered it.

But then, it had been some time. He had never been the jolly sort, not like his cousin Leif, who laughed more than he spoke. And there had been little to divert him from Fithne's betrayal. Only the usual battles—and yet one more reckoning he intended to take out of her hide was the fact that she had taken away some shine from the swing of his blade, the taut grip of his bow.

That was for later. Here, now, he laughed.

"Such a soft and lovely entreaty," he mocked her. "And such a comely voice indeed. It might even have worked, were you not wearing the very disguise you thought would keep me from you. What mercy I might have for your beauty is only a memory. Alas, I am unmoved by an old crone with stained teeth, no matter what voice she might use."

She shivered in his grip. He felt her swallow again, and liked it. And he watched as she blinked a few times, letting him know that she was trying her best to think her way out of this. At her sides, her hands curled into fists, then released.

He waited. Now that he had found her, he could wait as long as it took, because he knew now that her surrender was a foregone conclusion.

It always was.

"How did you find me?" she asked after a moment, her voice thicker. Rougher.

"Did you truly believe that you could hide from me?" Ulfric pressed his thumb gently, but firmly, against her pulse as it leapt against her skin. "Did you imagine I would not search for you forever?"

"I hoped you would be cut down in battle." She lifted her chin in his grip, though it pleased him to note she still did not fight him. "I prayed for such a boon. To your gods and mine."

He laughed again. "Your god abandoned you a long time ago, Eithne, and well you know it. Mine are far harsher masters. More demanding. They require better proof of your devotion than a paltry prayer. As you have learned, for here do I stand before you, unharmed."

"Every man falls," she said, and he still wasn't used to the sound of her voice. It was a possibility he never would be. It was huskier than he had imagined it. And she spoke the same Irish he usually did only with his kin, reminding him of the land he had called home when he was a boy. "It is but a matter of time."

"It is a great tragedy for you that my day has not yet come." He reached over and tapped his finger next to one of her eyes. That impossible green, far brighter than the finest spring. "Your eyes, Eithne. You can hide everything else, but you cannot hide them."

"You were not in the market." It did something to him, beneath his ribs, that she would fight him even now. However pointless the fight. It confirmed that he had not been wrong to imagine that this kind of fight was what he'd seen in her gaze all along. For she had never been as silent as she had pretended, even though she had not spoken. He had seen too much in the green of her eyes. They had ever been the loudest part of her. "If the King and his men had condescended to appear it would have been the talk of Jorvik."

He found he was stroking the column of her throat again, heedless of the stain on her skin, and it seemed only to bank the fires within him. Never extinguish them. Ulfric doubted anything could. She had gotten skinny in her time away, and he did not like that at all. But her throat still fit his palm, her chin resting between his thumb and forefinger as if it was meant to do so. His were large hands, nearly able to wrap the whole way around her neck, and well had he always liked it. He had held her thus from the very first day. After he had bought her, he had held her just so until she settled. Until her breath came normally and the glaze of terror faded from her gaze.

Until she had heaved a deep sigh, then given herself over to him.

He had used it ever since. Sometimes from the front, sometimes from the back, but always the same firm grip. Always, he waited for her to shudder, then sigh.

Then surrender.

If there were anything sweeter, he knew it not.

He could have told her that it had been his practice

since she had cut him to find a local boy each morn and promise him coin in return for scouring the crowds for any hint of green-eyed women. He could have told her that she had been spotted on her first day here and that he had nearly dismissed it—until it had occurred to him that as Loki himself came in so many disguises when the god so wished, so, too, could a deceitful woman find a way to hide herself in plain sight.

And Ulfric might have been one of the King's favorites, his face and deeds known well, but he, too, was capable of taking to the shadows and waiting for his quarry to show herself. Or he would not carry a bow as feared as his sword. He had but waited, then followed Eithne and the true crone who was her companion as they'd made their way back to a crude dwelling on the outskirts of this messy place. Still, so changed was her appearance that it was not until he had seen her response to the man of the small house that he'd known for certain that it was his own woman before him.

Eithne had obviously been helping prepare the evening meal within. For she had come outside to throw scraps to the dogs when the drunken man of the house had presented himself.

As he watched, everything in Ulfric had stilled. Everything had given way to that focused intensity that served him so well on the battlefield. Everything had gone quiet. And sharp.

Because he knew that look that the supposed old crone had thrown the man as he staggered toward the hovel, singing tuneless songs of men far braver than he could dream of becoming.

Ulfric knew it well.

It was the disdain. The hatred.

He would know her anywhere.

Then she had opened her mouth. Words had come forth. She had *spoken*, and he had been glad that he had kept himself to the shadows. For it had taken every bit of control he possessed to keep from roaring down the cluster of dwellings around him—

And he could not put his hands on her in anger.

For he did not wish to harm her—that could not possibly slake his fury nor his driving need.

He wanted nothing less than her utter surrender.

The next day, he had watched again, this time from inside the tent put up by a nearby merchant, who was only too happy to keep quiet. For it could only be a good thing to be owed a favor from a warrior of Ulfric's renown.

Ulfric had heard Eithne speak again and again. Once more, he had been pleased that he had waited to confront her, because there could be no confusion the longer he waited. There was no mistake.

Her betrayals tangled together. Her lies only grew thicker as he watched, as he waited.

And Ulfric could have told her all of this now, for he finally held her before him once more and would not let her go again, but he did not.

Better she should worry. Better by far she should wonder.

"Ulfric…" she began again.

But he only laughed again. He traced a finger from her temple down to her chin, then up again, and he knew the exact moment she understood that he was drawing his own scar upon her. Her eyes widened. Her breath caught.

"It pleases me to hear my name on your lips, little slave." And he let his gaze do what his hands would not, not here and not when she was so deliberately filthy. He let his eyes travel over the form she'd hidden away so well. But he knew. He might have to feed her up, but he would have *her* again. Her plush curves, her wide hips that had always cradled him so snugly. "Though I will like it far better when you call me by a different name."

He felt her pulse kick. Her green eyes widened. Even her breath took on a ragged sound. "I…I don't…"

"On the nights I cannot sleep," he told her, as if confessing a secret, "I lie awake, thinking of your misdeeds. Of how you deceived me from the start. I thought of the time you spent on your knees before me. The challenge I sometimes saw on your face. And I would have sworn to any who would listen that your surrender was complete. That you gave me all I demanded, then more. But you and I know the truth, do we not?" He ran his finger along the seam of her lips. "That you bit your tongue to keep from saying a word, and in so doing, betrayed me from the first."

"When you bought me in a slave market," she gritted out, as if she thought those words might shame him. "Not, I think, the heroic act you would have it."

"But you know as well as I do there were any number of fates far worse for you that day." His voice was grim. He kept his gaze trained on hers, and hard. "And hands far rougher than the one that even now holds you fast."

Not gentle, perhaps. But then, Ulfric knew she did not want *gentle*. Back when she had no voice to argue with, he had learned the truth of her in that silence. In the songs her body sang to him, again and again.

"You deceived me," he said, a condemnation all the harsher for the quiet way he said it. "From that very first day."

"You are mistaken," she said, but her voice was shaky now. And he could see her feelings in the way her eyes teared up, valiantly though she fought to blink the moisture away. "I hoped that if I was damaged, I would not be sold. That no one would want me when there were so many other girls whole and healthy."

Ulfric almost laughed at that. At her innocence in imagining that any man might reject a woman's beauty because it were silent. There were many who would consider that a boon better than gold.

But this was no time for laughter. He shifted his hand at her throat, just a little.

Just enough.

"Then say it," he ordered her, in that tone of merciless command that had always made her flush.

She did again now, and he was impatient already with this disguise of hers. For though he could feel the heat that suffused her, he could not see her bare skin as it pinkened. As it told him her true reactions.

It felt like one more betrayal.

"Say it," he commanded her again. "Call me what I am."

And he waited, staring down at her, pitiless and uncompromising.

For here, too, did he know the right weapon for the battle at hand. Here, too, did he understand that while any woman might bow her head to him, then submit to his authority as was only right, it was not enough. He craved surrender.

And not only surrender. He liked the taste of it from a proud woman, whose meekness sat on her but poorly.

He waited, for he knew that while she fought the inevitable—her struggle even now all over her face— her woman's softness wept for him. He knew that beneath her layers of rags, her breasts stood proud for him, round and full.

Ulfric knew this woman, inside and out. He knew the graceful line of her naked back in the firelight, bending her forehead to the ground so he could take her from behind. He knew how she looked with his hands wrapped in her hair, making it a knot while she knelt before him, her mouth filled with his cock. He knew how her face contorted as she rode him, her back arched and her breasts thrust before her like a Valkyrie while he held her wrists fast behind her. And he knew the sharp sting of her teeth in his flesh, biting down hard as the fire took her again and again.

Proudly had he worn those marks, even though he knew now she had bitten him to hide her voice.

And very likely because she had wanted to fight him, too.

Ulfric had no shortage of women to warm his furs. To yield before him with soft sighs and sweet whispers. There were always camp followers that tagged along from battle to battle. There were always hot-eyed women in the King's court, eager to try out a warrior's second sword in the dark. There were any number of women ambitious enough to take his cock the way he liked to give it, but none of them were Eithne.

Eithne, who had looked at him but numbly when he'd rescued her from that slave auction, for no matter what she might have told herself since, every other fate available to her that day had been grim. Eithne, who he had guided through the crowd of rough men, his palm at her nape.

No woman who chased after him could ever be that girl, stunned and disbelieving, who he had taken to the dwelling he'd claimed as his in the Dublin he and his kin had reclaimed. He had led her, without a word, to the wooden tub kept before the fire. He had undressed her, slowly, noting her terror. Then he had placed her in the warm water to bathe her with his own hands.

Carefully. Thoroughly.

And when he was finished, he had dried her off with a length of wool and set her down to kneel between his legs before the hearth. First, he had brushed her hair, and when he was finished, he had held her there. His hands wrapped around her throat from behind, holding her fast between his legs with the heat of the fire on her face, so she need not control her expressions.

His Eithne, whose shoulders had shaken for some while, then had stopped. Eithne, who had let out a long breath, and then, by degrees, relaxed in his hold.

Eithne, who had surrendered to him without a word. On her knees in Dublin that first time, relaxing into his hands. He had not pushed her. He had not treated her roughly. He had waited until she breathed normally again. Until her body lost its trembling, its watchfulness. Until her shoulders settled, her color returned, and she let out a long, soft sigh.

He had treated that moment—her helpless trust— like a blood oath.

He had taken care with her.

And he had kept his vows.

Thus did he wait again now, here in another crowded space, while her pulse rocketed beneath his hand. He waited while her green eyes were glassy, while her lips parted, while her skin grew hot and slick.

He waited until she let out that breath again, long and deep.

Until her shoulders fell and her hands were no more in fists.

"Who am I?" he asked her, with quiet intensity. With deadly heat.

Eithne let her eyes fall shut and her head dip forward, bowing it as much as possible while still in his grip.

"Ulfric," she said quietly. Her surrender near complete. Her chest rose, then fell. Her eyes fluttered open, the green there his undoing, as ever. And then she gave him what he craved. "My master."

Chapter Three

Eithne had dreamed this so many times. Caught, captured—and every time, every night, it had seemed so real that her waking had been a shock. She'd started to think that she ought to have been able to tell that the dreams weren't real, for they were too vivid. Too intense.

But now it was actually happening. And the truth was that she could feel all of this even more keenly than any dream. All of *him*. There was no red haze, or not only that red haze. Everything was a mad clamor, inside and out.

Only this time, she could use her voice.

Then, she had hoarded it like treasure. It had been the only thing she kept, the only thing that was hers. Sometimes when he'd left her in his tent, she would whisper to herself, old songs and stories she'd learned at her mother's knee. Soft memories, all hers, like her voice was, too.

Now, it had not occurred to her to bite her tongue.

And Eithne could not help but feel it were as much a weapon as the dagger she wore at her thigh. Hers to wield as it had once been hers to keep hidden.

Challenging him in the only way she could, then and now.

Ulfric released his grip on her neck and stood back from her, something in his dark gaze making her knees feel weak. Making her want to press her own hands to her throat, and not because he'd hurt her and she craved solace. It would have been simpler, surely, if he'd hurt her. Or if she could crave such things a regular woman might. But instead, there was that demon in her that she didn't understand, that she had never understood, that wanted nothing more than for her to sink down to her knees before him right here in the Jorvik mud.

The word *master* felt like a sin upon her tongue, but not like shame. And it was not as bitter as she'd expected.

Not when he looked at her the way he did now, as if he could see all those sinful places within her, all the wickedness he'd taught her, that had lurked inside her since she'd escaped from his clutches. All of it now bright and hot and *his* again.

It was almost a relief when he pulled her from the wall, binding her hands behind her with the length of rope she knew well he tied to his belt for this very purpose. And after he'd tied her wrists together, he paused, and Eithne knew he was remembering the same things she was, then.

The games he had played with ropes. The things he had made her do. Ulfric had a particular fondness for tying her hands behind her like this, then making her kneel before him, naked while he was clothed. She would beg him, as best she had been able with no voice, to pull out his thick root that she might suck on it.

He had liked that game too well.

And these were the secrets she'd kept all this time. These dark horrors. She had let Osthryth think that he had hurt her in the usual manner, when it was far worse than that.

Eithne had not hated these games.

Admit it, then, she ordered herself now. *You* liked *them*.

Every day since the morn he bought her she would wake, disgusted with herself, and vow that *this* would be the day his sorcery would not work upon her. Every day she would tell herself that no matter the steady way he gazed upon her, as if he knew her soul better than she did, she would stand firm against his wickedness.

She never had.

He had made her do so many terrible things and her true shame was she had trembled with need, not fear. There had been that raging fire between her legs, and even when she knew that he intended to make her kneel and use her mouth on him without his touching her at all, that greed had still come upon her. Ulfric would laugh and keep her knees apart, so she couldn't squeeze her thighs together and find that treacherous joy on her own. And when he finally deemed her supplication sufficient, usually when the heat of it all overcame her and trickled out the corners of her eyes, he would let her lick him slowly. Then work her way along his heavy shaft, always at his direction, until her mouth and her throat were full of him. He controlled it all—the depth, the pace—for her hands were bound helplessly behind her and she had no choice at all but to give herself over as a vessel for his pleasure.

Here in an alley in this crowded city, she could feel his hands on her arms and knew he remembered it all as she did.

And yet Eithne had known that if she told Osthryth a story like that, to illustrate what had been done to her as this man's slave and concubine, the older woman would have crossed herself and ranted about the evil acts these Northmen wrought.

Maybe that was why she had never shared such details.

Because the most frightening thing about Ulfric wasn't that he could have killed her at any time with his smallest finger. It was that nothing he had ever done to her had ever felt the least bit evil at all.

When Eithne knew too well that the priests would say nothing that felt that good could ever be naught but wicked.

Here, he pushed her before him, making her walk on her own feet as he guided her through the crowded settlement. Away from the crude dwellings where she had stayed with Osthryth's kinsfolk, past the busy market square where the trading was ever brisk, and into the part of Jorvik where she had never gone.

Deliberately, for all knew this was where the King's hall sat, with its view over the place where both Jorvik's rivers met and the old Roman walls that yet stood, like memories stout and yet squandered. People long gone and forgotten, though their work remained.

The first thing she noticed was that it was less crowded here. There were longhouses in the style of the Norse and Danes, as well as the smaller houses in the local Northumbrian manner Eithne had seen in villages out in the countryside. She kept her mind on the far grander dwellings here instead of the fact that as he walked with her, there were too many eyes on her and a chorus of whispers following them as they went. For thinking of those differences was better, surely, than feeling too keenly the way her heart ached.

She should have been used to these losses by now. One after the next, and surely there would be worse ahead. If she were a better Christian, the way she had been as a girl before the Northmen came, she would have taken her solace in the notion there would be a better life waiting for her when this dark one was done.

But she was a wicked creature who had fallen to her pagan owner, and there would be no better life for her. Eithne knew this all too well. She had only this one, as wretched as it might have been.

She had glimpsed Osthryth in the crowd as Ulfric

marched her off, bound before him so all could see her. The older woman's dear face had been bright with fear and Eithne had looked away, not wanting to call attention to her friend. Not wanting Ulfric to see her. But now, as Ulfric marched her down a wider road, where too many Northmen milled about in their red and blue cloaks—all of them too big, too broad, more like mighty oaks than men—she wanted to sob. To scream out her loss and pain as it ravaged her.

Because Ulfric had not hurt her, but that was before. And even if he somehow chose not to damage her now, that was the best she could hope for.

Eithne would never see her friend again. She tried to come up with some way to make that a lie but could not. And Eithne found she was not ready for this rough parting. She was not finished with the life she'd found out in the wilds of this place Ulfric had brought her to, the deep forests, the magic of herbs and roots, bark and flower. The nights she and Osthryth had spent together, making their simple meals and sitting out beneath the night sky, just the two of them.

Free and unfettered in this world where women were more often tied up or held down, as Eithne was again now.

She was not ready, but she had never been ready. Not for that dreaded day in Dublin, when the city had been in ruins, the fires still burning, and Feargal had come for her. Not to save her, as she'd foolishly imagined first, but to use her for his own ends.

Eithne had not been ready that day. To be sold, then bought, and shortly after taken away from everything she knew. For she had never returned to her old life. She still didn't know who had lived and who had perished that she loved. Ulfric had kept her confined in Dublin for two moons. And then she had been packed up onto one of his fearful ships and taken to Northumbria, so he might take his ease in her between his many battles.

She hadn't been ready for any of that. She hadn't known how easy it was to think herself a decent girl one day, only to know herself fallen the next. She hadn't understood that people lived like this. That they lived *through* this. She knew now that life carried on no matter how broken it felt and that sometimes, too, it was neither as dark nor as dire as it seemed from afar. It was made up of these sharp, aching moments that never seemed to end. When she didn't know how she would manage it. When if it had been up to her to breathe, she would have fainted dead away where she stood, never to be revived. But then she breathed anyway, and carried on.

There was no being *ready*, she thought now, as she deliberately chose not to meet the curious gazes of the people they passed. Because she recognized some of them, and she did not wish to think of them as *people*. They were Northmen. They were a scourge.

And anyway, they could hardly recognize her, dressed as she was in the tattered rags of a poor old crone.

Ulfric propelled her into a small house, though far nicer than the one she'd been sleeping in of late. There was a central fire, but his bed was up off the floor. There was wood everywhere, proclaiming his power and position.

And most men would treat a runaway like her roughly, shoving her so that she would fall, unable to catch herself with her hands bound as they were.

But the true treachery of Ulfric was that he was not rough. Or not that way. He was...*harrowing*.

Why should he abuse her when he knew he could make her ruin herself *for* him?

Again and again and again.

He closed the door, and there was only the dim light within, from the banked hearth fire below and the light from the opening in the roof above.

She could hear an alarming noise and it took her long moments to recognize it was her own blood loud in her ears. She stood just inside the door, holding herself stiffly, as Ulfric moved around very much as if he had forgotten she was here.

Eithne knew well he had not.

He was behaving this way to discomfit her. Too well did she know the games he played.

But despite herself, despite how long she had been away, the game had the same effect it always did. It was as if every part of her stood alert. Not only the parts of herself he had so thoroughly claimed, but she could also feel a prickle at the nape of her neck, that weakness in her knees, a faint trembling all over.

She told herself it was sheer terror at what he might do to her, though she knew the truth was far darker.

For she had led as blameless a life as anyone before his people had come back to Ireland, sacking and pillaging their way from Waterford to Dublin. There had been great sorrow after she'd lost her family, but surely there was ever sorrow. She had kept the house as her mother had taught her. She had done her best to be obedient and good to her brother. She had expected she might marry some day and keep her husband's house, and raise babies, too. It should have been a good life, a decent life.

But Feargal had sold her, this Northman devil had bought her, and she had been naught but wicked ever since.

For even now, she knew she was not as afraid as she ought to have been. For too surely had he woven together fear with that red greed, and though her mind told her to take care, that glowing heat in her woman's flesh craved whatever he might do.

For Ulfric had taught her that too, with his inventive punishments for trespasses he sometimes made up simply because the punishments amused him. Some nights she had lain awake, secured beneath the heavy weight of his arm and the ropes he loved so well and bound her in so tightly, and had fervently wished he would behave like the rest of his savage brethren. That he would use his fists, that he would take her so brutally it would leave her broken, so there could be none of this treacherous longing that ever made her hate herself.

She had understood from the start that he knew that, too.

Eithne had thought that pretending to be mute would act as some protection, and perhaps it had aided her in some things. She had taken pleasure in it. But too often did she think it had made everything worse with him. More intense.

For one thing, he had stopped asking her questions, for there would be no answer, and in that heated quiet between them there were only his commands. His stated desires that became hers. Perhaps she had made it easier for him to work his devilish will upon her.

And in all this time since she'd escaped him, she'd told herself so many stories about how she would behave if she could do it over again. How she would comport herself, for surely a decent woman would have found ways to stand up to him. To fight, even knowing she could only lose.

Surely virtue was its own reward, no matter what he might do.

Ulfric stoked the fire, and when the flames grew, indicated the heavy pot set over them.

"Water," he told her.

Eithne tried her best to remember what it had been like in these moments, when the silence stretched out between them and his commands had been few and far between, but she found it all blurred together. It was as if the only thing she could remember from her first round of captivity were the unspeakable things he made her do in his furs.

And not who she'd been between when he was not reducing her to that driving greed, that endless ache.

She didn't move, though she was aware that he did. She didn't have to look at him to feel him, everywhere. *This*, came a voice from inside her. *This was what it was always like, in between. Him, always. Him, everywhere.*

Her awareness of him had been all encompassing. It had been her primary pastime. She told herself it was survival.

And so it was again, she told herself stoutly now.

He moved behind her and released her from the ropes, and she hated that she did not feel any relief. Instead, it was as if she felt some sense of loss. Some disappointment that all he did was loosen the ropes, without touching her. Without taking her—

Surely not.

"You not only stole my property," he said in his silken way from behind her, close enough that she was sure she could feel the blazing heat of him, almost there, at her back. "You look as if you have damaged it irreparably."

Perhaps it would have been wiser to remain silent, even though he knew now that she could speak. But then, perhaps it was this that she was learning, if too late. That she had never been wise. That she had never been anything, really, until these men made her come to know herself. Her father by dying and leaving her unwed, and unprotected, though it was a likelihood that any husband she might have had would too have been slaughtered when the Northmen came. Feargal could have kept her safe, but instead had bartered her away to protect his own head. Maybe it had always been inevitable that she would end up in this Northman's hands.

But Eithne had now had the taste of what it was to choose her own steps, to walk her own path, and she could not pretend otherwise.

"I claimed myself as my own property," she told him, not sure how she dared. But once she began, it felt easier. Better. *Right*, something in her vowed. "If you wish to claim me, why can't I do the same?"

"Did you pay me the gold I offered for you?" came his voice, and if she wasn't mistaken, as the flames from him seemed to lick all over her, there was a dark amusement somewhere in there. It made the red heat in her seem to glow. "I have not been reimbursed, to my knowledge. Nor do I recall any bartering."

"It was my brother who stole me from my father's house and sold me to the slavers. Any claim you have for some kind of recompense you should take up with them." She shot a look at him. "Back in Dublin."

"I merely stole back what was taken from me," he said, and then he was circling around her, and that was different. Harder, certainly, to keep her chin up, when everything in her yearned to curl forward, to bow, to kneel. "You are my property once more. And the balance is not in your favor."

He reached up and she watched, not sure if she was fascinated or horrified as he traced the scar on his cheek. The mark she had left upon him.

Something deep inside her seemed to shiver, low and hot.

"It is a dangerous business, the keeping of concubines and slaves," she said after a moment, though her voice was the rougher for that shivering within. "I always heard tell it required a heavy hand."

"As you will soon discover," Ulfric promised her, the very picture of dark menace.

The decent girl she had been, once, might have wept at that. But the girl he had made her only shivered all the more, deep down, where no one could see.

And never with fear. Only with wickedness.

He tossed her a bit of wool and nodded toward the pot at the stove. "I wish to see the extent of the damage. Strip off these rags, for they offend me. And once you are no longer bedecked like a filthy beggar woman, you will wash. With soap, as I know you Christians despise. And then we will discuss recompense, Eithne."

There was no yielding on his hard face, or in his dark gaze. She stood there a moment, fighting to keep her breath even, as he pulled over a wooden chair, then sat himself in it. He stretched out his legs before him and crossed them idly, in case she was in any doubt that he was at his leisure.

Her fingers twitched. She stared at him. And she could not seem to move.

This was not at all how she had imagined it, all this time. His dagger was a heavy weight beneath her dress, and she longed to pull it forth and lunge at him—but she knew too well how it would end. And worse, even if she decided she did not care how it ended as long as she at the least *attempted* to fight this, she could not seem to make herself do it.

"I would not suggest that you make me repeat myself, little slave," Ulfric told her, his voice a dark warning. "You will like it little."

And as she stood there, gazing at him and his pitiless face with that fire in his dark eyes, it was as if at last a mist lifted and she could see all the other times he had made her stand before him thus. All the other times she'd had to forgo all she'd ever learned, all the grace and modesty her mother had imparted to her, because this game of Ulfric's was life or death.

Even when it did not feel like it.

And never had a game been more life or death than now. Far as he sat, one finger moved over that scar, reminding them both that she had taken his own blade to his flesh. Reminding *her* that when she had thrown herself out of that tent near Corbridge, she had expected to be caught and killed on the spot.

Had there not been a war going on she would never have escaped, and she knew it.

That day, all she had wanted was what she'd gotten.

Away from him. Eithne had not thought beyond it. She had not let herself truly believe, in the light of day, that she would ever be in this position again.

But it is ever thus, came Osthryth's voice in her head, far wiser and full of worldly things than Eithne's sweet and simple mother had ever been. *Women wield their power in different ways than men. But sooner or later, for the world is ever wicked, every woman must find herself outmatched by a man's strength, whether he be good or bad. And better she should use her wiles than the alternative.*

What is the alternative? Eithne had asked while huddling in her threadbare cloak, out near the fire in that cold wood. *Are there truly any alternatives?*

But you already know, my girl, the old woman had said, her gaze kind. *For here you sit, unencumbered by any man, and well do you and I know this is not a woman's natural state.*

The priests would tell us we are not natural, Eithne had said. *And what is not natural must be wicked, must it not?*

Though she shouldn't have cared if she was wicked or not. For it was a certainty that she was fallen and long lost, sucking the bones of the woodland creatures they'd managed to trap and living like that, her hair free in the night air and her body her own.

The old woman had cackled. *I listen to priests in church*, she had said. *Where they are the experts, or so they say. But out here?*

Eithne could still see her careless shrug.

And she thought, staring at Ulfric's ruthless gaze, *I know how to do this.*

She had survived him once. She could survive him again—for she could see that the very same fire that had singed them both then still burned bright in him.

Eithne would survive him once more.

And she focused on that—not that traitorous leap of a hard kind of joy within her at the notion of surviving him at all. And what that might entail, day by day.

Because what came with that but the impossible pleasure he forced upon her, that in all these days apart from him, she had never managed to forget.

But she risked his impatience here. And she knew better than that.

He had taught her all too well.

So Eithne took up the cloth. She dipped it in the water warming at the fire and lathered it well with the soap she knew was made of fat and ash and pleasing herbs. And then slowly, painstakingly, she revealed herself to him once more.

Chapter Four

She was different now.

At first, Ulfric did not care for the difference. He misliked any sign of real change in her, including the rags she wore to deceive any who looked upon her. But here in his dwelling, beneath the thatched roof where the open fire danced over her face, he found he liked this new Eithne better every moment.

For he knew who had taught her to look at him this way, from beneath her lashes. He knew who had showed her what her hips could do as she moved them this way and that, shrugging out of the ragged and dirty cloak, revealing garments much cleaner beneath. She wore a simple apron and woolen dress as any peasant woman might. He looked more closely at her dress and the leather shoes on her feet and saw the signs he'd missed in his fury over her rags and filth. She was not dressed in the fine clothes he had demanded she wear when she was in his possession, but the plain things she wore now were well-cared for. He could see the evidence of her neat stitches all over her dress and apron, making certain the fabric lasted.

Lies within lies, that was Eithne, but Ulfric had been raised the son of warriors. Well did he like cunning in a woman.

For he had found that such cunning ever led to a wantonness in his furs.

His cock stirred and keeping himself in check grew more painful with every breath, especially when he knew he had no intention of slaking his lust upon her just yet.

Not just yet. There was far more reckoning due between them.

And first he had bade her wash herself, as these savage Christians so hated to do. He had heard tell their own priests forbade it, and while he did not believe all the stories people told about them, he had bathed her the last time he'd taken possession of her, too. And he had introduced her to the ways of his people, who washed each morn and kept themselves clean and well-groomed at all times, for who could say when the day could end? Times were brutal, as often as not, and who wanted to spend eternity dirty and unwashed should the Fates cut the strings before nightfall?

It occurred to him that though she looked filthy, she did not smell it. Another indication that this was all a part of her grand deception. Ulfric decided it would better serve him if he viewed it as a performance.

Eithne took her time washing her arms and hands,

slowly revealing the fair, creamy skin he recalled so well beneath. She pulled off her apron, then the thicker woolen dress beneath. He noted that she pulled it from her body awkwardly and more, that it landed on the floor a bit more heavily than it should have—telling him what she concealed—but he stayed where he was. For she was wearing only a rough linen shift now, and he was hungry for the sight of her after so long. For the sway of her breasts beneath the thin fabric and the tempting shadow between her thighs.

Everything in him seemed to coil tight around a single word. *Mine.*

For even standing there before him, scrubbing off dirt and lies, her hair naught but a mess of ash and deception, he wanted her. He had wanted her while he bled. He had wanted her across the seasons since. He should have wanted nothing more than to strike her down for her treachery, but he did not. He could have punished her in the usual ways, by maiming her and disfiguring her for both cutting him and running from him. A slave must ever bear the brunt of any treatment he dealt out, whether as punishment or for his own entertainment.

But though the law would support him in any number of brutal penalties, the simple truth was that he did not wish to look upon this woman with her beauty forever marred.

Still, Ulfric comforted himself with the knowledge

that though he did not intend to take her hands or her life for her theft, the ways he wanted her were…not soft.

He had always been a hard man. His brother Thorbrand, a winter his elder, was the more moderate and cool-headed of the two of them. Thorbrand had ever been better suited to games of chance and courtly intrigue, and served their King well in that regard. Ulfric had mastered his blade and his bow, and had no patience for anything he could not control the same way.

He had sworn his fealty to Ragnall when he was but a boy, and he kept his oaths. But he bowed his head to no other man, and it was well with him if all others trembled before his wrath. He won friends in battle, not by playing courtly games in halls or captivating the company with songs.

Let others sing songs about him, Ulfric had always held. For weak men feared him and strong men looked him in the eye, and he had no doubt that when his time was up, it was to Valhalla he would go—and happily.

And he knew what the women said of him, their whispers and warnings. Just as he knew that there were some whose soft lips parted at the sound of those very warnings. Those who looked at him anew, a different interest in their gazes, when they heard the rumors of what nights were like in his furs.

Yet better than all of them was his Eithne, his very own, who had come to him an innocent. And thus he had crafted her with his own hands into a woman who met every one of his specifications, in his furs and out.

For he was no less exacting about the things he wanted from his concubine than he was about the state of his sword, the responsiveness of his bow.

He watched now as she scrubbed the last of the dirt and stain from her face, and though there remained a hint of it yet sunk deep into her flesh, still he could see her beauty revealed.

He could not have said if it enraged him or inflamed him, or if it was some combination of both. But he could not look away. And she knew it, for her green gaze met his.

One breath. Another. Only then did she reach down and pull her shift up over her head, revealing herself to him at last.

And the monster he kept within him, chained tight, roared then. The hunger he carried with him always grew sharper. Deeper.

He lifted his hand and drew a lazy circle in the air with one finger, and did not allow himself to smile when her eyes spat fire at him.

Fire or no, she obeyed him. She circled around so he could see that while she needed fattening up, to better take him in all the ways he intended to have her, there was still a greater offense. For her flesh was not only clean and pale where she'd hidden it away beneath her rags, it was wholly unmarred. Ulfric preferred her with his fingerprints on her, his marks all over her, and he had taken great pleasure in making certain there was always proof that she had been taken well and thoroughly.

Eithne had not only escaped him—she had erased him.
He would enjoy making her pay for that.

"It pleases me that you have taken no other," he told
her in a growl when she faced him straight on once
more. "I will factor it into the penalty you will pay."

He saw her eyes widen, then heat. While the same
time, she swallowed hard. Ulfric did not have to see
the goose bumps rise along her arms to know that she
was caught somewhere between longing and concern,
exactly where he liked her.

He watched with interest as her chin rose in that defiance he still liked too well. "You cannot know that.
Perhaps you taught me your form of swordcraft so well
that I must practice it constantly. A woman must survive, must she not?"

Ulfric was a man of great appetites, and unlike some
he knew, he generally encouraged the same appetites
in others. Women and men alike.

But not Eithne.

"I taught you to crave only me," he reminded her.
Yet he remained in his seat, lounging there as if the re-
covery of his errant property were a casual thing. As if
he might have happened upon her by mistake. It would
not do to give her any airs. Already the women whispered that he had treated her too well. Less like a slave
and more like a treasured steed, by their reckoning. "It
would not surprise me if you had put this to the test,
having cut me with my own blade to secure your escape and having come to Jorvik where you must have

known I have made my home for some while now. With such brazen audacity, what would you not do?" He said it all quietly. Mildly. And he could see that his words landed on her like stones. *Good*, he thought, and continued. "Still, I doubt it, for well do I know your hunger, Eithne. And the marks it inevitably leaves behind."

Her green gaze turned hectic, and her lips turned down. "Your perversions may have marked me, but that does not mean I liked it."

Ulfric allowed himself a small smile then, the smallest curve of his mouth in one corner only. "It was not the marks on you I meant. But rather the ones on me, little slave. Or have you forgotten your own perversions?"

He could see she didn't like that at all. She looked away, which had once been as good as turning her back on him. He had not allowed it. He had punished her when she defied him and did it anyway.

But now it mattered less that he could not see her gaze. He knew how to read far more of her now, thanks to those first, silent years. And it didn't matter what she felt or what she thought today. It might never matter to him again, so intense was that sense of betrayal and his need to take it out on her in the way he liked best—though he could admit that he intended to find out, all the same.

For now she could tell him. In words, should Ulfric determine that she should. Whether she cared to tell him or not.

Maybe the change in her circumstances impressed

itself upon her, because she did not wait for him to remind her how little he'd liked her turning her face away.
She looked back at him, her gaze stormy.

"I assume you wished me naked so you might slake
your lust," she said, almost primly. As if she was not
so much offering herself but sacrificing herself, and
he laughed.

"You look like a beggar by the side of a muddy road,"
he told her, shaking his head slightly "I do not take
women caked in dirt and grime into my bed, Eithne.
Well do you know this. So too do you know what to do."

He waited then, watching her fight with herself.
She looked torn. Clearly wishing to fight with him but
thinking better of it.

And he was well-pleased when she turned back to the
hearth. She set up the basin for washing and then knelt
there, ladling water into her tresses, lathering them with
his soap, and then combing them clean with her hands.
He liked it that she did not pretend not to know what
he wanted.

Just as the monster in him liked that she would smell
as he did now, of that same soap. And soon enough of
him, too. And as she knelt there, her thick hair around
her like a shroud, he took the opportunity to investi-
gate the pile of her clothing for the source of that thud
he'd heard.

Quickly enough, he found the dagger she must have
been carrying on her hip.

His dagger.

And Ulfric couldn't decide if he was pleased that she had kept it all this time, close to her body, like a truth she wanted to keep secret even from herself. Or if he was outraged at her arrogance, that she would carry this clear evidence of her thievery with her.

Either way, he retrieved it and tucked it back where it belonged on his belt. Then he sat in his chair again, studying the way she presented herself to him as she washed her hair at his command.

There was that fury simmering in him, as ever, that she had dared run. That she had betrayed him in such a fashion, and in doing such, had taken this from him. The simple pleasure of watching her move about before him, wherever he lay his head. He took a particular joy in watching her do the things all women did, but for him. And at his specific direction, for it made the whole of their life together a part of the great, dark joy he took in her in his furs.

The joy she took in return, little though she liked to admit it.

He had allowed himself to trust her softness, thinking it had swept away her cunning. It was a mistake he did not intend to repeat.

Eithne sat up then, squeezing the last of the water from her hair. And she had forgotten herself, he saw, for her gaze when it found him again was nothing short of insolent.

He would need to retrain her.

And everything in him roared again in the face of

such a dark, encompassing pleasure he had not imagined he would live long enough to experience again. This time, he did not intend to be as patient. Nor as understanding.

Though he almost laughed at that, for he doubted she would call him either.

"Burn your clothes," he ordered her softly.

He watched her calculate. And wondered, idly, how she planned to either conceal the fact she had his dagger, or perhaps even wield it. She'd cut him the once, sure enough, but that had been different. Ulfric did not intend for those circumstances to repeat themselves. Ever.

And surely she must know it. He saw her eyes flicker and then she turned, her hair a sodden tangle down her back. But glossy and black once more, pleasing him anew. She moved over to the floor where she had dropped her rags in a dirty heap and swept them all up into her arms, lifting them all as one and turning toward the fire—

She was good, he would give her that. He saw the hint of a frown appear between her brows, but there was barely a hitch in her step.

"Are you missing something?" he asked her.

Eithne fed her pile of clothing to the flames, one garment at a time. She did not toss the bundle on top of the fire, potentially smothering it. She knew well that was not what he wished, and so stood there, naked and damp, her face averted as she concentrated—so virtuously—on carrying out his commands.

She could not have shown him a more perfect indication of her guilt if she had tried.

"A dagger, perhaps?" he continued in the same mild, almost careless fashion.

"I have returned it to you," she said after a moment. He caught the quick green of her gaze as she flicked a look at him, then returned it to the fire. "For when I take a person's property, *I* know that it is stealing and *I* hasten to return it."

He pulled the dagger out again then and set it down. On the floor beside him, there where he sat with his back to his sleeping alcove, a far cry from the tent where she had abandoned him. And in this house of timber, where so many opportunities to indulge his imagination beckoned from all sides. But that was for later.

Now, he only looked back at her, daring her.

He could read her indecision all over her. He could see that part of her that urged her to simply lunge forward, to go for it—because either way, it would be over then.

His poor little concubine. His wretched slave. She kept imagining that it would ever be over.

That he would ever let her go.

She was breathing heavy enough that it made her breasts bounce gently. And then her gaze sharpened. She lifted her chin, as if accepting that having found her this time, he would always find her. That even though more than a year had passed, he had never stopped looking.

Nor would he.

And never had he seen a woman prouder, or more glorious. Her naked flesh, scrubbed and sweet-smelling, gleamed in the firelight. Her black hair was a glossy fall over her shoulders that teased at the dimples above the curve of her bottom. A perfect place to grip her, he had ever thought.

Ulfric could remember too well the sight of her at the slave market. She had stood in only her shift, leaving nothing to the imagination. Her eyes had been glazed over in the way a slave's often were, as if to distance themselves from the shame of their situation, even in the wake of battles like the one that had still left Dublin in flames. And Ulfric had no need of slaves. Women begged for the opportunity to be his concubine. He was no farmer or merchant, always in need of hands for labor. Nor was he, like some rich men, riddled with the need to show off his status.

Ulfric knew his worth, and well. It was in the swing of his blade, the accuracy of his bow. The weight of his gold and the favor of his King.

Like any man, he wanted sons, and for his tale to be ever told, ever sung. But he had fought his whole life with honor and courage, and he knew well that his deeds would live on after him.

Someday he would wed, when he was an old man and could sit by the fire singing songs of glory to his aching bones. Until then, he would fight, or he would fall, and he would worry about sons later. For Ulfric had kinsmen aplenty, and tales of his bravery did even now honor their names.

Yet he had stopped at the sight of her, standing there in the market that day, looking something like tranquil in a sea of so many rough men who wished to celebrate their victory with a woman who could not divorce them. For they had vanquished the Irish Kings, taken back what was theirs, and now wanted a warm sheath for their swords at the end of the day, and better still, a slave woman who could see to all their needs now the long campaign march was ended.

Ulfric did not need to buy a woman to fetch his water, not when so many offered to do it for no more than the hope of his pleasure.

And yet there was something about Eithne's stillness that had called to him that day, straight to that darkest need that lived within him, the one he dared let out in full only sparingly.

Very sparingly indeed, though it was never enough. The monster in him rattled its cage and was never satisfied.

Ulfric could not help but admire the way she stood there that day, looking oddly calm in the face of what was happening to her. All around her, other women had sobbed and wailed and recoiled as their fates were traded for gold and coin from far-off lands. All around, the men had jostled and laughed, boasting of a different kind of swordplay and their own supposed prowess.

Still, she had been calm. The kind of calm a man

like him dreamed of and had no hope of finding, not in this life.

But he did not take slaves, particularly not as a concubine. For there was no greater pleasure than a woman surrendering to him because her body willed it and wanted it, even as her mind and heart fought. Of all the battlefields he had known in his time, there was none greater or more satisfying, though he dared not say such things where other men might hear. He regretted only that he had known it so little—only pieces, here and there, as he honed his favorite craft but could never fully sink into it with women he had not trained.

There was no fun in taking a slave. He craved surrender by force of need, not law.

The crowd around her had grown louder and one drunkard pawed at her, making her flinch away from his hands. Though she had nowhere to go, with the slave trader holding her arms behind her.

And Ulfric would have normally admired the pretty picture she made, then carried on.

But she blinked, and for a moment, that distant gaze of hers had changed.

He had seen a flash of that wild, bright green.

And better yet, fire.

He'd felt it in his cock, as if she already knelt before him and took him in her mouth, never using her hands to manage depth, the power. Surrendering to him again and again and again.

Ulfric would have sacked Dublin all over again to have her.

Here in Ragnall's Jórvik, she only called to him the more.

Because he already knew.

He did not look at her and hope he could call out that mix of defiance and desire, he already knew it lived in her. He already knew well that she was fashioned, every bit of her, to make him long to lock them away somewhere and dedicate himself to nothing but the passion between them.

But men did not rest when there were kingdoms in play. Warriors could not slumber, nor go soft, for that way, they might as well kneel before their enemies and offer up their blades. He ever had work to do, whether it was maintaining his position in Ragnall's court or the simple, daily practice of swinging his sword and shooting his bow.

Still, he had plans for her.

"Do you take up this dagger again this day?" he asked her, the rough growl of his voice loud in the tension between them. "Next time, better you should aim for my heart if you wish to do me any damage."

He saw that fire dance higher in her green eyes, and still it pleased him. Deeply. But it pleased him even more when she spoke.

"I will confess I did not know you had one," she said, almost sweetly.

He wanted to laugh, but did not, for he did not want

her easy. Not today. For he had spent a great deal of time considering exactly what he would do, and how, when he brought her back. All the ways she would pay, each more pretty than the last, until he was satisfied.

And Ulfric was never satisfied.

He swept up the dagger and enjoyed the way her gaze tracked his movements as he tucked it away once more. Then he rose and was pleased by the way her eyes widened in apprehension, as they should

He moved over to his bed and pulled out the staff he kept within reach. It was stout and long and he tossed it slightly, then tested the weight against one palm, fully aware of the way she watched him do these things from behind him.

Fully aware, too, of the way she caught her breath.

"I would not advise it," he said. Then he turned back around to see her two steps closer to the door, a guilty look on her face. "For they would set upon you in the streets, naked as you are. They already whisper that you must be a *huldra*, sent to lure unsuspecting men and bewitch them. I would have to fight my own kin to retrieve you, and this, little slave, I would not look upon with favor."

"I thought that was to be my fate." He could see the difficulty she had in keeping her voice even. Or almost. "Is that not the punishment men mete out most? Is that not how women are punished? Used crudely by too many, until something inside them is broken. So many rough and careless men, heaving heedlessly to grind her down to dust. It is only a wonder you have not shared me out already for your men's amusement."

Ulfric moved toward her, the staff in his hand. Though she tried to keep her head high, he could see the way her gaze followed the staff, no doubt remembering the kiss of it against her skin.

"Life is harsh and brutal," he said, pitilessly. "This is true everywhere, Eithne. No one is special. We are all of us in danger of being taken down by one blade or another. Who is to say which cut is the deeper?"

"Yet there is one battlefield where only the men are armed," she retorted, as if she couldn't help herself. As if finding her voice had made her reckless—or, then again, perhaps it was only the fear of finding herself back here again, when she had blooded him to get away. "The same men who sing songs about honor and raise tankards high in mead halls are naught but cowards in their furs. Such brave warriors indeed, to hold a woman's hands above her head, and wield their little blades unchecked. What would happen if every woman had her own dagger at the ready, and men must take their chances for a change?"

Ulfric only considered her a moment. "Do you truly think a woman unarmed?"

Though once the words were spoken, he would have taken them back. They revealed too much.

Her chin rose. "I know the only time I held a dagger in my hands, I also found my freedom."

"If that is how you wish to tell it," Ulfric said, with a shrug. "Anyone might sing a song, little slave, but the gods know well whose tales are true and whose are but stories to while away a dark night."

And this time, when she flushed, he had the great pleasure of watching the pink of it move all over her, so that even the rosy tips of her breasts seemed darker, duskier.

His mouth watered.

But first, discipline. Or she would be impossible and, sure enough, he would bleed again.

"You remember the staff." He held it out between them, and gloried in the delicate flare of her nose, and the way her shoulders moved, as if the breath she held was too great for her form. When he waited, she offered only a quick, abrupt nod. "If you look closer, you will see that it is no longer as smooth as you recall."

She kept her gaze trained on him for another moment. Only then did she look more closely at the staff. And more, at the notches that lined it in neat incisions into the wood, stacks and stacks of them, covering almost the whole of the staff itself.

"A mark for each day you stole from me, Eithne," he told her, his voice low. Rough with his fury, raw with desire.

Her gaze snapped to his, and everything between them turned to flame. Everything between them was white-hot, the ache of it so intense, he almost looked down to see if he had accidentally placed his hands on the hearth.

"Why…?" She swallowed and he watched, greedily,

the way her throat moved. "Why did you make a note of such things?"

"Oh, little slave, I think you know."

And he never tired of studying her. The way the pink of her skin deepened to a telling red. The way goose bumps rose along the line of her neck, over her shoulders and down her arms. And best of all, how the heat between them made her sweat.

He inhaled and could scent her arousal, as unmistakable as the way his cock pressed insistently against the fabric of his trousers. This dance of theirs, as if it had never ended. Nor ever would.

"One strike for each mark," he told her softly. His own rough poetry. And he set the staff down where she could contemplate what it meant for her, what it would do to her. How it would make her feel. "A mark for a mark, if you please. You already know you must earn your pleasure, I think. And so you will again."

"I want no part of your pleasures," she threw at him, though her voice was thick and the color high on her cheeks.

"You may lie all you wish," Ulfric growled. He took her face in his hands, holding her to him and digging his fingers into the wet silk of her hair. He hauled her close, and everything in him sang. For she was beautiful, and she was his. And her body told him everything he needed to know. Here, where he could show all parts of himself. Here, where he could let loose the need in him only she had ever met fully. Here, where they could explore the passion between them with no end. "Perhaps you have forgotten that your greatest lie was pretending you had no voice. You gave me no option but to read your thoughts all over your body. Shall I tell you how it sings to me?"

"It is only flesh," she threw at him. "And wicked though it may be—"

"Never doubt that your soul is mine, too, little slave," he said, his mouth at her ear, then brushing her temple. "For I own every part of you, in this life and the next."

Everything in him longed to plunder, to pillage, to sack the temple of her mouth, her body—but he held himself back, for he knew that waiting made it better.

Or worse, for her. But all the sweeter for him.

He dropped one hand to find her throat and he held her there some long moments while she fought to breathe normally and failed. She tried to throw her daggers at him with her gaze alone, but failed there too, for he saw the heat gathered in her gaze. He saw how it made the green there all the brighter.

Ulfric waited, feeling her hands wrapped around his wrist here, his forearm there, her nails digging into his skin. A glance down showed him that she stood high on her toes, her whole body straining, more beautiful than he had dared recall.

He thought he might die if he did not get inside her.

But there was a reason he stood at Ragnall's right hand. And it was not because he fell at the first sign of battle.

He waited, until her eyes closed. Until she heaved a great breath.

Until she relaxed into her surrender the way she always did.

Only then did he move her over to his bed, lifted up from the floor in its own alcove, a mark of his status. No pallet on the floor, like the one he had seen she'd shared with that crone she'd traveled with.

He could feel her heart pound, and it pleased him. Once he'd laid her out on the bed, he pulled out the ropes he had prepared for her here and carefully, almost tenderly, tied her wrists. One to each side of the bed. Then he stood back to admire the picture she made, her hair the kind of messy he liked best, her eyes bright and furious, and her naked body begging for his touch in all the ways it always did. Her nipples hard, her flesh pink.

Ulfric had missed her. He had missed this.

"I hate you," she threw at him.

It sounded convincing, but he could see how hard her nipples were. He bent down and took one between his thumb and forefinger, pinching her hard enough to make her gasp, though she tried to stifle the moan that followed.

He said nothing, only traced his hand over the ribs he could count beneath her skin, a reminder that she had left him to scavenge about like a witch in the woods… But he shoved that outrage aside as he found the indentation at her waist, the soft curve of her belly, and then, better still, the thatch between her thighs.

Only then did he lift his gaze to hers as he slid his fingers through the coarse black curls to find the truth of her. Her woman's flesh, stiff and proud, and all around, the honey of her need. He raked his fingers through her folds, watching her closely for her reaction.

And it was as beautiful as he recalled it, that war in her between surrender and fury, while the truth was in his palm, melting hot and soft.

He squeezed just hard enough so that she could not contain her moan that time.

Ulfric stood back, pleased. He cleaned his hand with his own tongue, tasting her for the first time in far too long, and liked that it made her press her thighs together. It nearly had him tearing off his clothes and pounding into her, like a man possessed, but he held himself back.

Barely.

"There's nothing I want more than to lock myself away here and discuss your deceit until you are little more than a puddle at my feet," he told her, his voice dark with the force of his hunger. "But mine is not woman's work, roaming the forests digging for roots."

She yanked hard and bared her teeth when the ropes only tightened. And he watched as she clearly thought better about kicking him.

He almost wished she had.

"For always there are wars that men must wage," she threw at him, not bothering to hide her scornful, disrespectful tone. "Else how could you justify the things you do?"

He only laughed at her, though it was a question he had asked himself upon occasion. It made him miss his brother, gone across the sea, for Thorbrand had often wondered if there was more than sword and King and these endless squabbles over lands and kingdoms, bloody forever.

"Hold your tongue, little slave," he told her. "For now that, too, is mine. And soon enough, you will learn what you should already know. That whether you use it or not, it will be my pleasure, not yours."

Ulfric did not tell her how it was for him now, to hear her speak. How much more intense it was between them, because he could not only see the truths her body told him, she could tell him herself. In the words she chose, in the way she threw them at him, in all the ways he had wished—before—that he could know her.

He had hated losing her, but she had returned to him with even more gifts than before.

Ulfric would take his pleasure in each and every one of them.

He made himself turn then and leave her there, naked and furious and tied to his bed, so she could think about what she had done.

And better yet, contemplate the staff he left propped up at the foot of the bed, a stark promise of what was to come.

Chapter Five

Ulfric stepped out into the summer evening with a song in his heart.

And found his cousin waiting for him on the road where so many of their brothers in arms had set up their houses once Jorvik was theirs. There were animals roaming in the yards behind the houses, children in the street. Women carrying pails of water in from the rivers, and the scents of life in close quarters, from cooking fires to the sharper smell of cloth being scoured and dyed, the blacksmith at his forge, and the variety of preserving practices to make sure there was meat all year.

Leif was a battering ram of a warrior, with the red hair of the Norsemen in their blood, not the black Irish who marked Ulfric and Thorbrand. He was known for his big grin, his booming laugh, and his ability to bring any man foolish enough to challenge him to a drinking contest to his knees. Ulfric knew him better, however. He knew that Leif had made himself indispensable to their King not for his capacity for ale and song, but for his cleverness. For Leif alone had the power to lull enemies into a false sense of safety. He had drunk with wild Scots. He had made the Irish Kings laugh as they'd chased Leif's own kin from their shores.

He could charm his way into anything and out again, too.

As such, Ragnall used him as a spy. Yet not for Leif the sneaking about or shaving off his beard to pretend he might be an overlarge Saxon. Leif walked in tall, laughed loud enough to make any hall seem tiny, and still managed to finesse Ragnall's enemies into telling him their secrets.

Today, his cousin was smiling, his blue gaze knowing as he took Ulfric's measure. "There are rumors all over Jorvik. That Ulfric the Ever-Scowling and Eternally Grim found himself a beggar woman by the river and has turned his smiles upon her. This can only be witchcraft, cousin. I have come to rescue you from the old crone's spell."

"What rescue did you plan from out in the street?" Ulfric asked, arching a brow. His cousin only smiled wider. "You said I would never find my runaway concubine, yet I insisted I would. As ever, I had the right of it."

Leif let out a laugh at that. "I hear she has aged, cousin. My memory of your concubine is that she were comely, yet it is said you took a crone from the market square."

"There is no mortal trickster greater than a deceitful woman," Ulfric said, sounding grimmer than he felt in truth. He clapped his cousin on the arm. Harder than necessary, because he felt like it, and it made his cousin grunt. "But she will learn the error of her ways, this I promise you."

Leif laughed again and fell into step beside him as Ulfric started for the King's hall. "It is good you found her, for you know what they say."

"Do we listen now to the jealous whispers from lesser men?" Ulfric asked, and he let his voice carry, there in the street where there were always ears pricked, ready to take his words and play with them like the wind.

For he knew well what they said. He had told Eithne the same. Ever seeking to drive a wedge between Ulfric and his King, they whispered of Ulfric's obsession with his lost slave when surely he could but replace her—for what was the difference between one concubine and another? They liked to whisper that it was witchcraft, or weakness, that kept a scowl on his face to match the scar a mere slave had left him. They liked to claim that it rendered him unequal to the task of defending his King.

He had always answered those whispers with his sword. With the carnage he brought in Ragnall's name on battlefields from the Isle of Man to Northumbria, Corbridge to Jorvik. Whispers could do as they liked, but his sword told only truths. His bow brought only honor.

But Ragnall had taken Jorvik. The Mercian Lady had at last been defeated and her daughter cast out by her own uncle. It was rumored that he had killed her himself, for none had heard her name mentioned since. Edward of Wessex had not taken kindly to his sister's defeat and had liked even less Ragnall's domination of the Christian Danes who had attempted to hold Jorvik. He had been certain that Ragnall could not hold Jorvik when his sister had failed to do the same.

Yet hold it Ragnall had.

And it was these times of supposed peace that held a greater danger, Ulfric sometimes thought. For a proper battle had its clear opponents. A man either swung his sword or did not.

These whispered campaigns, murmurs sly and lies dark, were enemies far harder to fight. For what good were the songs a man had sung about him if there were too many whispers when he walked? Ulfric preferred monsters he could smite down with his own hands. His palms itched the urge to do just that as he and Leif made their way along the road, weaving their way in and out of the crowds that were ever thick as they approached the hall where Ragnall ruled on matters great and small. Some peasants walked for weeks for a chance to lay their woes at his feet and ask for surcease.

"It is not what we listen to that matters," Leif said as they walked. He moved nimbly, belying his size, around a pack of dogs fighting over scraps. "But whether or not such whispers reach the ears of our King and cast you in their shadow."

"If my King does not prize my sword, if my deeds do not make my vows shine the brighter, then listen well he should to the lies of the jealous," Ulfric declared, untroubled.

For there were dangers when warriors spent too long in the softness of a mostly peaceful city. Training each morn was no substitute for the reality of the long march, the bloody fight. And there were always those who entertained themselves with petty gossip—usually because their tongues were their only blades.

Yet he knew his King was canny. He was a direct descendant of Ivar the Boneless, who had made these cold islands tremble in fear. And Ulfric had proved his worth and his fealty too many times to count.

He had the gold to prove it.

As he and Leif walked through the early summer's eve, the small boy who had found his errant concubine in the market in the first place ran beside him, trying to match their strides. Ulfric tossed him a bit of silver, beckoning him close.

"Half of that is for your trouble," he said in a low voice. "And the other half is yours, too. All you need do is watch over my dwelling. If any dare enter, sound the alarm."

"It is done," the boy said fiercely, looking at Ulfric the way he knew he had once looked at Ragnall. Then the boy took off back down the muddy road, as if he would defend Ulfric's threshold with his own hands, should it come to that.

It was a short walk to the castle Ragnall had claimed when he'd taken the city and had made his own in the year since he had sent the Christian Danes running. Leif and Ulfric walked into the hall together, calling out greetings to their friends and companions in arms who already filled in the seats at the long tables. The women bustled this way and that, filling cups as the evening meal already bubbled on the hearth, smelling of rich game as befitted a king's household.

Ragnall himself sat at the head of his table. His beard and head were turning to gray, yet there was no doubting the power he wielded. Whether seated at his table or leading his men into battle, his was a might that could not be denied. His clever gaze moved over Ulfric and Leif as they approached and he waved them to take seats beside him, as the others around them moved good-naturedly enough. The women brought them ale and Leif leaned in to tell a story of the traders he'd met with in the marketplace today and the stories they had brought of lands far distant and their kin abroad, fighting the warlike tribes who battled as men did here, sending their traders north for honey, wool, and female slaves aplenty.

"Leif tells me there are whispers I must contend with, sire," Ulfric said before Ragnall could speak, because he had always preferred a good offense to the long, cold wait of any decent defense. "So closely am I watched that Leif would have it that all of Jorvik must be interested in who warms my bed."

Ragnall laughed. "She was pleasing to look upon, your concubine. It is no mystery that she might turn your head again. But it has never claimed your attention from more important matters." The King's laughter faded as he looked out over his men. "There will always be those who mistake their own weakness for ale and women to be universal."

Ulfric found himself fingering his scar and smiled faintly when Ragnall's gaze tracked the movement. "Revenge is sweeter, perhaps. But it will not be a sweetness to all involved, I wager."

Ragnall's eyes got very bright at that. He tapped his tankard to Ulfric's. "No indeed."

And they sat there as the rest of Ragnall's court assembled, the *skalds* sang happy songs of battles won, and the women came bearing drink enough for all and soon, platters of the rich stew that all might fill their bellies.

"Edward moves on the Danelaw," one of the men was saying from farther along the table. "He will not rest."

And were the greedy Saxon King to get his hands on the Danelaw, all listening knew, he would have no need to divide his attention between Ragnall to the north and the Danes to the east. He could focus his attention entirely on Jorvik.

"His first act after claiming Jorvik would be to either disrupt our connection to Dublin, or take it," Ulfric said.

Leif nodded. "How better to gather his forces and move on the Scots?"

"The bloody Scots," someone else muttered, and they all offered an oath or two to that, though Ulfric did not think he was the only one who would not have minded a skirmish or two, even with the savage Scots to the north, simply to test their blades after too long only swinging them in training exercises.

"I await word from Sitric even now," Ragnall told Ulfric later, as the *skalds* sang of the King's great bravery when he had ruled the Isle of Man and all his men sang along, pounding fists and cups upon the long tables as they belted out the words. "The channel between Northumbria and Ireland must remain strong. And I may require a more personal messenger this summer, while the winds are in our favor."

Ulfric nodded. "My sword is yours, My King," he said, and he meant it. As he always had. "However you wish it swung."

And he found he enjoyed the evening in the hall far more than he had in a long while. For he was replete not only on the food and song, but he also knew what waited for him in his bed.

For it was certain there was no better peace than this, he thought. Especially when his King had just reminded him that no peace ever lasted. For at any time he might well be dispatched all the way to Ireland at Ragnall's behest, and who knew what dangers lurked along the way? The woods were filled with wolves. Bandits ever gathered along the waysides. The seas were uncooperative even in summer, and the gods did like their little games.

There was no warrior alive or dead who had ever

bested the Fates, nor ever would. No man lived a moment more than planned, king or beggar or any in between.

He thought of this later as he headed out into the summer night. Jorvik smelled of cooking fires and the leftover warmth of the day. He could hear the river in the distance, and from all directions he could hear men singing, the sound of a city well-defended. The dark was only beginning to creep in as he walked, for Midsummer approached and with it the longest day of the year, heralding the beginning of the long, slow slide into winter.

Last year he had marked Midsummer with a scar on his face and a stone in his heart. Ulfric had found no peace in the hall, no ease with his kin. He had heralded the coming of the winter cold with only his betrayal to warm him, and he had marked the long nights one by one on his staff, dreaming of her return.

Now he could put those dreams into action.

At last.

When he reached his dwelling, the small boy waited there and stood quickly when he saw Ulfric before him. He squared his shoulders, like the man he would become one day. Ulfric nodded, tossing him a parcel of bones he had picked from his stew, that the boy might suck out the marrow.

The boy's eyes widened in gratitude. He clutched the parcel to his chest. "No one dared come to your door. No one came near."

Ulfric considered him. "And did you go inside?"

The boy looked stricken. "I would never!"

"Good lad," Ulfric murmured gruffly, and waited for the boy to run off with his bounty.

Only then did he push his way inside. And found before him the very vision that had danced in his head all night. And all the more succulent for the anticipation.

It was as he had pictured it so many times. Eithne where she belonged, with ropes on her body, secured to his bed, flushed with temper—

And far more than temper when her eyes lit upon him.

He could see the fire in her. He could feel it in him.

Ulfric did not greet her. He busied himself instead with shrugging off the day. He took out the portion of stew he had brought with him and set it near the hearth, that she might smell it. He sat down to remove his boots and unwind the lengths of fabric he wrapped around his legs. He put away his weapons, making sure they were in reach of both the bed and the chair. His reach, not hers. Then he stripped down to his trousers, for the habits of a lifetime of camping on this battlefield or that were with him always. He liked his spaces neat and clean. He kept his weapons close, for there was no telling when enemies might rise—even from within his own bed.

As he took off his cloak and tunic, he examined both for tears and stains, for he usually handled either immediately. He was no Saxon savage who lived in one garment until it rotted from his body, and he had tunics and cloaks to spare—but he took good care of what was his. Always. Tonight he found no stain or tear needing his attention. He hung out his clothes before turning back to his beautiful slave, trussed up before him, and took a moment to appreciate the sight.

Because he not only took care of what was his, he liked to enjoy it.

Particularly when it was Eithne. He liked greatly the way her eyes seemed drawn to his bare chest. Ulfric was sure he could feel the green all over him, like her clever hands. He threw his braids back over his shoulders and crossed his arms as he stood over her, letting her eyes widen at the sight.

Though it was not a true panic that swept over her, red and bright. He would wager it was only a very little measure of panic at all, mixed in with the wanting.

"I hope you enjoyed this opportunity to think of your trespasses against me, little slave," he said after some while, when her cheeks were like bright red flowers.

"I thought a great deal about trespasses against you," she gritted out at him.

He wanted to laugh at that, and the continuing gift of her voice, but he kept it within him. For there was no time, now, for merriment. This was a serious business, his and hers. And it was well past time for the repayment of her debts.

"You know I like your defiance too well," he told her quietly, though he could see she did not mistake it for softness. "Better still, you know precisely how it is repaid."

Her eyes blazed and she gripped the ropes tighter, pulling them taut.

But all he could note was the way that position made her arch her back, so her breasts were thrust forward.

And he had eaten the King's game this eve, yet she was the more tempting morsel.

"Is this a part of my punishment?" she demanded. "That you stand before me and threaten me, doing nothing but talking at me?"

"You will know when your punishment begins, Eithne. Anything else that occurs you can assume is all for my pleasure."

It should not have been possible, but that red shade grew brighter. In her cheeks. Down her neck. Even across her belly. "If you were any kind of man, you would think less of your pleasure and more of a woman's. Instead of these twisted little games you like so well."

Ulfric settled himself beside her on the bed, his mouth curving as she tried to roll her body away from him. He let her do it, because who was he to keep her from these empty victories? It would make her eventual surrender all the better for both of them.

"But you and I know the truth, do we not?" He reached out then, hooking his hand around her far hip and hauling her back toward him. And, once more, he watched her wisely choose not to kick him as she clearly wished to do. "It is these twisted games that bring you the most pleasure. It is the very wickedness you claim to abhor that brings you joy."

"You are nothing more than a devil," she threw at him.

"'Tis not the devil in me you fear, little slave." Ulfric tightened his grip on her hip, just enough to make her breath catch. And her flesh heat. "But rather the devil in you. What you truly hate is that I know it."

She opened her mouth, clearly intending to snipe at him further. But he forestalled her by smoothing his hand up over her belly to her breast. He cupped the tender weight in his palm, then found her tight nipple. He tugged at it and her breath left her in a rush.

"You are afraid of this devil," he continued, his voice low. "It chased you from my furs. But then again, it brought you back."

"That is naught but your Northman arrogance talking." Her voice was thicker now. And he would wager she was red more from her hunger than her temper, just then. "I would never have come here, were the choice left to me. But unlike some I could name, I think of others. And if Jorvik was as peaceful as so many say, it made no sense to stay away. Osthryth has enough now to trade her way into a warm winter near a fire. Do you truly imagine you could have anything to do with that?"

"I know I do," he replied, his attention moving from one plump breast to the other. "Because I know you. And I know that no matter what stories you tell yourself, little slave, the truth is that you could not stay away."

"You love to call me that," she hissed at him, because she was hissing out a breath at the way he pinched her nipple. She struggled against her ropes, so he pinched a bit harder. "You think it makes you the victor. But all it does is remind me how much I hate you."

"What it does, Eithne, is remind you who you are."

He leaned closer then. He angled himself over her body, still pinching her nipple, close enough now so that he could hear the faint squeaking sound she made an attempt to swallow, back in her throat. There had been a time when that noise was like the sweetest song to him.

But now there were better songs to sing.

"Mine," he told her, in case she was confused. "You are *mine*."

"Yes," she managed to get out, though her voice were much fainter, and her eyes far brighter. "That is how slavery works. But do not delude yourself into thinking I like it."

"I know you do not." He propped himself over her then, letting even more of his weight press her down into his furs. She shuddered, then her body relaxed— until she clearly felt her own telltale sign of surrender and stiffened again. "I know, and you know too, that what you truly hate is how well you love it."

And before she could mount a new fight, he put his mouth, hot and open, to the crook of her neck.

Ulfric tasted her pulse, and how it kicked back wildly against his tongue. Then, taking his time, he began to move south until he found her nipple with his mouth, and sucked it in deep, even harder than his fingers could pinch.

So that she arched off the bed, making a shape like his bow.

"You say you do not like the devil in you," he said, his attention on her sweet flesh. The heat of it. The softness, like the fine silks the traders from far away sold here. He made his way down the length of her, then settled himself between her legs. "But I do."

He leaned in and breathed deep, her arousal making his cock ache. Then he took her softness in his mouth, because he wanted the taste of her. He wanted her on his tongue. He wanted her writhing beneath him, her hips bucking up to meet him, the pleasure too much to bear.

Ulfric licked his way into her, then took that greediest nub between his teeth and raked it, just enough that her heels dug into his back as she lifted herself up, quivering all around him in a way he knew meant she was *this close*—

And then he stopped.

He sat back, watching her closely as she slowly came to understand that he did not intend to toss her over that edge. As it dawned on her that he was but toying with her.

"Did you forget who we are, little slave?" he asked, his voice a dark rumble between them.

"I forgot nothing," she threw back at him. "But you surely love nothing so much as these cruelties of yours."

"Yes, yes," he murmured, almost as if he pitied her.

"It is a cruelty, is it not, that I dare to give you such pleasure."

"Your pleasure," she corrected him, her eyes glinting that green fire he craved. "I merely suffer it."

He stayed where he was at the foot of his bed, still kneeling there between her widespread legs. And he wondered if she knew what a liar she was. For he had taught her not to close her legs unless he bid it, and surely if she hated him as much as she claimed she did, she would not be obeying him even now.

Without so much as his finger upon her.

"But this is the devil you fear above all others," he told her in that quiet way that he could see move through her, every word its own sharp cut. "That it is your own sweet suffering that leads to my pleasure. And that this, in turn, brings you joy."

"What would make me fair joyful would be if you let me go." But her voice was much rougher now. Her eyes were much darker and filled with winter storms. Because he had spoken only the truth and he knew his little slave did not like that. "You could have a hundred other women serve you just so. Only one word from you and they would line the streets of Jorvik to offer themselves to you. Why must it be me?"

Ulfric ran a hand along her leg then, pleased to find that there was strength in her. Even if all the walking she had clearly done had taken some of the lushness from her curves. He wrapped his palm around her ankle and watched the heat on her face betray her. For it was a certainty she was recalling the many times he'd secured her that way, too.

And all the games he liked to play.

But only with her did they matter like this. Only with her did they cut him deep, then make him better. As if all the playing he had done before had been a shadow, and Eithne the sun.

A truth he did not care to tell her.

"I expected to find you already taken more concubines to serve your needs," she continued, not waiting for him to speak. Likely because she knew she would not be happy with whatever he might say next. "Too well do I know that you like warm flesh in your bed."

Ulfric did not laugh, though he came close enough. "What man does not?"

"All men do not require it in the manner you do," she countered. She yanked at the ropes holding her wrists and he wondered, as he always had before, what she would do if she could strike him in truth as she always seemed to wish she could.

But he supposed he had his answer now. The scar on his face seemed to throb at that.

"And all men are not as twisted as you are, Ulfric."

He smiled down at her, but it was the kind of smile he knew well that women thought cruel, and it had its usual effect. Most women saw it and thought better of their coy glances his way.

But this was Eithne. It made her shudder and her eyes grow big. It made her nipples harden into greedy points while that red flush washed over her from head to toe. Better yet, the scent of her arousal grew strong.

She might call him twisted, but whatever was bent in him was gnarled the same way in her. They were crooked roots twined into the very same tree. He had known this from the start.

"All men are not as honest as I am," he corrected her mildly enough, though it made goose bumps rise on her skin. "Nor are all men as prepared to do what is necessary to get what they want."

"You mean buy it from a slaver with fists like hammers?"

"I do not mean that, Eithne. As I think you know. For any man can avail himself of the slave market if he can but afford it."

He stood, reaching out for his staff again, and held it before him. Then he stood there beside the bed, rolling it in his palms as he looked down at her unmarked body.

And he could see the anticipation in her eyes. Better yet, he could see the heat. The fire-laced green of her gaze seemed to spear straight through him, winding around and around inside his body until it held his cock in a noose.

"You have stolen all these days from me," he told her. "I promise you we will mark well each and every one of them."

He watched her closely. All of that green fire, but more, the way she shifted on the bed. He knew that were he to ask her, she would claim that she tried to get away. That she was testing her bonds and no more, but he knew better. What she was truly about was pressing her thighs together, because like it or not, she could not help herself.

She wanted him, and this dance of theirs, too badly.

Like it though she might not, Ulfric had known from the beginning that the two of them were kindred in this particular dance. This particular dark.

"Imagine if you found yourself on the slavers block," she said, her voice higher.

"Such a thing would never occur." Because only a fool would take a warrior of his caliber hostage, much less attempt to sell him. Assuming Ulfric walked off a battlefield instead of dying with honor, that was, in which case he might as well be a slave, for he would surely also be a coward.

She was still trying to weave her words around him. "And then, already made a slave, to be used thus. To be made to do these terrible things."

"It is terrible, I grant you," he agreed, as if commiserating with her. "To scream as you did, silent yet loud, from all that pleasure."

"Not always from pleasure." Her gaze was on the staff he held. "Very often not from pleasure."

"Behold the mercy I intend to show you tonight, Eithne." He waited for her to shift that wide-eyed gaze from the staff to his face. "For each mark upon this staff is an insult, and I will answer this insult by putting a matching mark upon your skin."

"How is that merciful?" she very nearly yelped at him.

Well indeed did he like that sound.

"You may choose the number," he told her, as if granting her a great favor. "But know this. I expect you to take responsibility for what you have done."

"For securing my freedom?" Eithne let out a wild sort of laugh. "I'm only sorry I did not think to plunge that dagger into your neck."

He let that same sense of betrayal in him swell as it would for a moment before biting it back. Then he wrestled it into a soft simmer and told himself it was temper. He waited for it to pass. For while he intended she should answer for her sins, temper was for a battlefield lined with steel in men's hands. This battle required a clearer head.

Ulfric was far too invested in its outcome.

Only when he was calm again did he incline his head. "The more you choose, the kinder I will be with each blow. The fewer you choose, the crueler the kiss of the staff against your flesh. The choice is yours. You may thank me, Eithne."

"That is no choice at all," she managed to say, now sounding hoarse.

Meanwhile, her green eyes were so wide that the dark centers nearly overtook the green. Her chest moved rapidly enough to make her breasts bounce, telling him that no matter what she said, her body was already taking her into those dark, crooked shadows they could only find together.

"Whoever told you that you would like what choices the gods see fit to give you?" he asked as he stood above her, drawing out the moment, the tension. Making them both ache with what was to come. "It is only children who expect the choices set before them must all be pleasant. And you and I are not children, little slave."

"I think you must mean boy children," she threw back at him. "For there was no girl child ever born who does not know from her earliest possible days that all of her choices come at a cost."

He tapped the end of the staff against his palm, taking no small pleasure in the way she pulled in her breath at the sound of the wood hitting his flesh. "Your words go around and around in circles. You bemoan your slavery, but surely you cannot imagine that any other road would be so very different. You are a woman, as you say. Whether you bow to your master or to your husband, what choices are your own? You must serve a man one way or another. Thank me, Eithne, for allowing you any voice at all."

"If I were a wife, I could divorce you," she snapped at him.

"You are Irish," he pointed out, and the steel in his voice made her pant a little, there before him. "Your Christian God would see you married for eternity."

His people had always allowed their free women

more leeway than the Christians did. And well should Eithne know it, having come of age in a Dublin that bore the marks of his clan.

"But you—"

"Enough," he said quietly. And liked it well when she went silent. As surely as if he had placed his hand over her mouth. "You cannot talk your way out of this, Eithne. Your words cannot save you any more than your muteness did. But then, we both know that truly, what you long for is not your freedom. But total surrender."

"Never—" she began.

"Eithne." His voice was like a blow then, hard and insistent. It stopped her, as he meant it to. "I tire of your games. Choose how many strikes you will take this eve. Or I will."

Chapter Six

The clamor inside of her was like a battlefield.

Eithne could hear steel clashing with steel, men's shouts and bellows of rage and pain, the thunder of feet and horse's hooves against the earth—

Yet well did she know that it was all within her.

"If you say you will choose no strikes," Ulfric continued on, pitiless monster that he was, "we will begin with ten. And I will not lie to you, little slave. You will find them onerous indeed."

Everything inside of her was shaking apart. Even her breath as it moved in and out of her mouth. For she knew he meant what he said. He kept smacking his own palm with that dreadful staff and every time he did, she could *feel it* in that soft place between her legs where he had already feasted on her tonight.

Feasted, then left her bereft. Deliberately.

For she knew too well that this Northman kept his promises.

All save one, came that dark voice within her that she refused to acknowledge. She shoved it aside.

And all he did was watch her as if he'd been turned to stone. Only his gaze seemed alive, lit up by these dark, encompassing fires that raged between them. Eithne knew too much this time. She knew him too well.

It had been different the first time, when she had interpreted anything that was not him kicking her into a pulp at his feet as kindness. Sometimes in this past year, she had wondered if that had been what twisted her. If she would no longer know real kindness if she stumbled over it—but no. For she had stumbled over Osthryth and had recognized her for what she was. A friend when a friend was sorely needed.

Tonight, Ulfric had been gone some while and it had allowed her to remember far too much about the kinds of things that had occurred in his furs, now that she lay in them once more. It was not as if she had forgotten, try though she might, but it had all run together over time. It had become mixed in with those dreams she had and the red, hot burn of it all when she woke.

Tonight, nothing seemed dull. Everything was sharp and hot and too close to painful. She could feel the weight of that staff as if he already pressed it into her. As if he held her down, the wood against her throat.

It shamed her that imagining him doing that sent a flood of heat between her legs once more.

Maybe he was right about the kind of marriage she might have had. For Feargal had intended to marry her off before the Northmen came, and what was to say his choices would have been better? At night while he was in his cups, he would eye her darkly as she moved around the small cottage she had kept for him after their family had all died, muttering about her beauty and how best it could serve him. Why had she thought that somehow, a marriage chosen by her brother would be any better than this?

Perhaps it would not be better, she allowed, if only inside her head. But it would not be *this*.

She'd seen more coupling as an untried girl than she would have wished, for so it was in Dublin, where enough people lived close together that there was always someone doing something in a place they should not.

Yet she'd never seen these games Ulfric liked so well. Though these were only games to him. Because she was the one who had to suffer for their pleasure. Already she knew—she remembered—that every touch of that staff would be like fire. And that he intended it be a debt she paid him and so would do none of the things he could do, if he wished, to make it better for her.

Because he knows you, came that voice she wanted to hear least. *And he may indeed wish you to submit to this punishment because he likes punishing you. But you would not respect him if he did not.*

That was another truth she had no wish whatever to face.

But she could see he grew impatient as he waited beside her, that fearsome chest of his gleaming in the firelight, and she had no doubt that he would do as he said. And choose both the number and strength that would hurt her the most. Because he intended to punish her, thoroughly.

He meant it when he said that she had stolen from him. That she knew and more, that it was not his dagger he had missed. Now Ulfric intended to take back what was his. Directly from her hide.

Perhaps she would never know what it was that was so twisted within her that some part of her thrilled to that notion. It had haunted across the past few seasons as surely as if it were a ghost, like the ones even the most devout villagers whispered they saw in the coldest months, slipping in and out of the shadows while the winter wind blew on.

"Ten," she threw out, for she could see the restlessness in his gaze and knew that if she did not do the very thing she wanted to do least, he would make it worse.

Because he always made it worse.

Before he makes it better, that treacherous voice within her whispered.

And she felt the blood within her seem almost to thicken too much, so loud did her own heart sound in her ears then. Because the smile Ulfric gave her then seemed to her to be pure devil. She could feel it everywhere, cascading over her, making her skin prickle and feel too tight.

He moved then, almost too much to even look upon, this towering mountain of a Northman. His whole body

shouted out his profession, his calling, his trade. He was
made of heavy slabs of sheer male power, and he wore
the scars of many battles all over his body. So many
scars that the one she'd dealt him seemed almost foolish in comparison, and yet she had no doubt that hers
made him the angriest.

For she had not scarred him in the kind of battle others had. He might even argue it had been no battle at all,
for she had taken advantage of his slumber.

When Eithne knew it had yet been a battle for her
very soul. And she was not at all certain that she had
won it.

For here she was, tied to yet another bed. Her eyes
were as wide as the flesh between her legs was damp,
and yet all she could seem to pay attention to was the
way he moved. And better yet, the outline of his male
weapon, thick between his legs.

She hated herself because even now, her mouth watered to taste him. Even though she knew that nothing
with Ulfric was ever easy. There was no tasting, no
tempting, without a price.

And she was ever the one who paid it.

He went to the ropes he'd restrained her in and with
a few hard tugs, released her. But only so he could pull
her up from the bed and stand her before him, taking
his time as he tied yet another rope around her wrists,
securing them behind her.

It was as if she was spinning. She felt herself go
around and around and around, like a child did to make

itself dizzy. Except this was no child's game, and she was already as dizzy as if she'd drunk as much as her brother always had.

And that was before Ulfric sat down on the bed before her and gazed at her a moment. He smoothed his hands over the front of her, now she was exposed to him so fully. He ran his palms over her breasts, pinching her nipples until she hissed in a breath. Then he followed the shape of her body down to her hips, and it occurred to Eithne that surely she should have felt shame in this, too. The intensity of the way he looked at her, as if he was inspecting her. Inspecting his property.

He was, she realized the next breath. That was precisely what he did here. For all of the things he did were about claiming her as his. Again and again and again.

She forgot that at her peril.

"Tonight you can make all the noise you like," he told her, and there was a dark current of victory in his voice then. It shivered in her, too. "You can scream, cry. Beg me to stop, if you like, for I will not." Eithne had always been silent before, though it had cost her. He had always done his best to make her break that silence, or so it had seemed to her, and refusing to surrender that last, treasured part of her had nearly ended her more than once. But now he knew better. The corner of his mouth moved slightly then, while his dark gaze seemed to bore straight into her. "Thank me for my kindness, little slave."

And lying there, tied up on the bed before him, she

could have argued forever. But this was different. He was so big, so commanding, and his hands were on her flesh. Her arms were tied behind her back, and her nipples ached, and she knew what was coming.

Eithne knew it was coming, and her body was already singing its mad little song. She wanted to call it terror, but she knew better. She could feel her own honey on her thighs. And already, she felt as if she had tipped off the edge of a high cliff and was even now falling, hurtling through the air.

His dark regard kept her aloft. As if without it, she would crash hard into the ground.

"Thank you," she whispered.

The curve in his mouth grew harder, somehow. "Thank you, who?"

And she would never understand how he knew. How he always knew. How he divined every little hiding place she had. Even when she had not spoken, he had found her.

He had always found her.

That part of his promise, he had kept.

"Thank you," she managed to force out again. And then, though it hurt, "Master."

Ulfric grunted a little. That was all, but it was like music to her.

And then his hand was gripping her hip, his fingers digging into the flesh of her bottom, as he hauled her toward him.

His mouth found one breast, then the other, while

his free hand found its way between her legs, handling her with the same exquisite roughness as his mouth against her nipples.

Finally.

Eithne's head fell back, her mouth opening of its own accord. Her hands, bound behind her, opened and closed, but there was nothing for her to do but take this. Whatever he gave her in whatever manner he liked.

Between her legs, his fingers played her like a lyre until she was pressing up on her toes, but not to pull away from him. Instead she arched her breasts even deeper into the torment of his mouth, then pressed her hips against his fingers, so big and rough, yet elusive, never quite giving her what she wanted—

Ulfric pulled away then. He reached up to hook his hands around her neck, holding her there, and she thought for a giddy moment that he might kiss her mouth—

But when she saw the flash of heat in his gaze, knew he wouldn't.

That was a privilege. Just as pleasuring him on her knees was a privilege. And Ulfric believed in nothing so much as earning privileges.

He tipped her over his lap and let her fall, and even though she knew that he would catch her, the rush of it made her belly seem to hollow out and hurtle on its own toward the floor.

Once tossed over his lap, she could not seem to think of anything but how she must look as she felt his hand smooth over her bottom, warming her skin. He moved his legs so that her toes could not brace against the earth, and held her there, helpless, her hair tangled all around her face.

But it wasn't until she shuddered out a breath and went limp that he began.

Not with the staff, but his hand. The first smack was jarring. It was not gentle. He was not easing her into this the way he had long ago. His hand was large and hard, and the rush of fire from the blow was immediate.

And it brought her back. It brought her here, thrown over his lap. Sometimes with her hands tied like this, other times with her hands free—though that was worse. Because he would demand in his deceptively quiet way that she move them out of his way and would punish her for it when she failed. And she knew too well that the true shame was not when she failed, but when she obeyed.

It brought her back to the press of her belly and breasts against his hard thighs. How he knew how to kick her legs apart so she could not do anything about the way the fire he built in her raced straight from her bottom to that place between her legs, and only seem to glow with every smack of his palm against her tender flesh.

He had spanked her daily. He had told her why. This was not a punishment, this was pleasure. His. Because he preferred that her bottom always be red. That she never sat easily. That always she should feel him, and always and ever she should remember who owned her.

I am a simple man, he had told her long ago, still in Dublin, on the morning after he had bought her.

The morning after he had held her in his bed, one hand tied to the wooden post with his hands around her throat, until she somehow fell asleep. And she had woken that morning shivering with a longing she hadn't quite understood. But he had.

That spanking had seemed brutal to her at the time, even though she had known, even then, that it was hardly more than a bit of tapping. Far lighter than the way Feargal had boxed her ears on occasion, simply because he could. And her brother had never taken that pain and made it sweet.

Ulfric had taken all that fire and sting and traced his fingers through the heat between her legs, then made her come apart.

Every day.

He praised her when she cried. He praised her the more it hurt. And he never praised her so much as when he pressed those rough, battle-hardened fingers of his into her heat and tore her to pieces, still tipped over his lap like this.

It had taken her a long time to understand that he had trained her thus. To want pain with her pleasure, that edge to any sweetness. So that by the time he took her maidenhead, the pain of that tearing, the shock of him inside her, only made her burst into flame. Then come apart beneath him.

In her time in the woods, she thought too much about these things. She thought about the way he had taught her and the way she had responded. She had told herself that being away from him brought her clarity. That she had gone along with him out of the instinct for survival all women possessed and nothing more. She had done what she must, as all women did, and the proof of that was that she did not crave these dark delights when he was not near her.

Surely if she was the kind of craven, abandoned creature she had always felt she was in his presence, she would need that same sinful release wherever she went. But she had not.

Eithne had started to imagine all that darkness in her, all that red-hot, crooked hunger, had simply been the means by which she'd gotten through her captivity.

Even tonight, she'd laid in his furs surrounded by the scent of him. The furs had abraded her skin as if it was his beard, marking her all over. And she had told herself that any response she'd had to him was shock at finding herself in his clutches once again.

No matter how good he smelled.

But finding herself tossed over his lap was a true reckoning.

For this was where he had always forced her to face the truth. The hard inevitability of his hand striking her bottom. Inerrantly finding the places that hurt the most and staying there, over and over, until she was squirming. Until she was out of her head.

Until it took the fiercest strength of will to keep from betraying herself by making those noises that would give her away.

And tonight, she realized what a gift that had been, to hold on to her little rebellions. To have something to wrap that core of herself around, so that he could not have it. So that he could not have *everything*.

For tonight she had never felt more naked.

He continued to spank her, his pace unhurried, his hands hard. Always so relentlessly hard.

The heat in her eyes spilled over, cascading down her cheeks.

"Beg me to stop," he urged her, in his pitiless way. "Beg me, Eithne."

But for so long she had clung to her silence. It had been her only weapon, her only retreat. For so long she'd managed it, though he had brought her to these places again and again. Some nights she'd bitten her own tongue hard enough to taste the blood, and that was the only thing that kept her from it.

She had lost that. It was gone. That bloody-mindedness, that bitterness—it was as if she'd left it somewhere in the dark northern forests.

And even as she told herself she would die before she made a sound, she could feel a sob rising in her.

For it was one thing to be betrayed by her brother, to be sold, to be taken. She'd survived her captivity and at the first opportunity, she had made her escape. But it was different now. It was much, much different to return. Without her silence to hold on to.

As if maintaining that silence had been her hope.

He had taken that from her today.

And yet she could not call it hopelessness that had her sobbing then the wild sounds coming out of her against her will, and then somehow shifting into words.

"Please, please, please," she cried.

"Please, who?" he demanded, his voice as hard, as intent, as his hand as it rose and fell without pause. Though far rougher than she had ever heard it before, as if this was as decisive a moment for him as it was for her.

And thinking so was how she could do it, in the end. How she could use her voice in this place where she had always nearly killed herself to remain quiet.

"Please, Master," she sobbed. *"Please—"*

But he did not stop.

If anything, he spanked her harder. And her sobs became a howl. And Eithne was as scared of her own passion, her own intensity, as she was amazed that all of this was within her. Had been within her all along.

And once again, Ulfric had known.

She was sobbing in earnest when he shifted from those inexhaustible blows against her bottom that felt red and inflamed and huge. He smoothed his way beneath, finding her dark fur and then thrusting his fingers roughly within her. While he let his thumb drag against the part of her flesh that stood high and cared not if it begged for him.

It was like that great redness was not only in her bottom, but inside her. It grew and grew, filling her up, almost terrifying her in its intensity. It grew and grew with every thrust of his knowing fingers, every movement of his thumb—

Until she burst.

And still he kept up his pace, his other hand moving to massage the globes of her bottom roughly, so there was the pain and the sting, mixed right in with the release, and it made her scream. Or perhaps that was only more sobbing, so tangled in and around itself that she could not tell the difference.

And it had never been like this. It had never been so good, and she knew it was that she could let out at last. These sobs, these sounds. All the storm and howl she had always gulped back, no matter what it cost her.

Her mad keening went on and on and on, until she realized that he was driving her up to another cliff and she was heedless, reckless, racing straight toward it when everything in her wanted to pull back and hide—

But she had no control. He simply pressed down hard, and she was lost.

Ulfric gave her no time to recover. He stood her up on her feet before him and held her there. That dark gaze swept over her, assessing her, and the cruel curve to his mouth told her he liked what he saw.

"Kneel," he ordered her.

Eithne felt her knees hit the ground before she knew she meant to move, her body already lost to him all over again. Her thoughts could not keep up.

He picked up the staff and held it before her.

And his gaze was its own command. She knew too well what he wanted. And so she leaned forward and kissed the staff, as he would have her do again when he was finished.

"Good girl," he murmured.

And Eithne wanted to hate herself for the wash of pleasure that moved through her, but she could not.

Ulfric reached over and pushed her hair back from her face, then curved that hard hand that smelled of her over her cheek. She wanted to think it a tenderness, but she knew better.

This hard man had showed her tenderness but once. And she'd cut him for his trouble. She doubted he would ever do it again.

And sure enough, he only held her face at an angle, so he could make her kneel up just enough to make sure she wasn't comfortable.

"Ten strikes," he said, in a voice that made the way he'd struck her bottom seem like a kiss. "You will count them off, then thank me. If you do not count, or do not thank me, we will start over. And no," he told her when she frowned slightly, "any extra strikes you earn will not count toward the total. Only the ten."

She stared back at him. And even though moments before her body had been weak in the aftermath of her first spanking in more than a year, that edgy pleasure still coursing through her, she was already beginning to quiver again, deep inside.

For she knew what awaited her.

"That hardly seems fair," she managed to say, though her voice was by no means steady.

"It is not meant to be fair," he returned with that maddening steadiness, and too much fire in his dark gaze. "It is meant to remind you who you are."

And it did.

He laid her out, making her kneel over the side of the bed, and he kicked her legs apart, so there could be no comfort in this. She could hear the staff whistle each time he swung his arm, for that was her only warning, though it mattered little.

Because it took her over. It didn't matter where he struck. On her bottom, two on each side, and she thanked him for the sheer brightness of each. On the tops of her thighs, laying two separate tracks, one for each leg, until there were three on either side.

"Thank you, Master," she sobbed.

And she could feel each and every one of them, like stripes of his favorite fire. The deep bite of each blow took her over. She knew the spankings were about training, and they were tied into this pleasure he insisted on forcing upon her. He had made sure to do it tonight, to remind her that when he pleased, he could make what hurt turn into something glorious. He had wanted to make sure she remembered it.

For this was precisely what he'd said it was. Punishment, plain and simple.

And yet in each blow, she was sure she could discern the full measure of how he truly felt about what she'd done, made all the worse for being tempered. For each blow was exactly like the one before it. Exactly like the one following. He did not give into the temper she knew burned inside him. He doled out the punishment she had asked for, one strike after the next

So that all she could think of were the many marks on that staff, and how he would make each and every one of them hurt, just like this.

It was overwhelming. It was meant to be. And yet, somehow, she managed to choke out the proper number with her thanks. As if this was her apology for leaving him. As if she thought she owed him such.

For reasons she did not care to explore.

When it was over, he did not shift it over into pleasure. He did not put his hands between her legs, to play with her until she sang.

Eithne had no notion of how long she lay there, crumpled over the bed, the sensation only seeming to grow inside her. She had no idea how long it was before she realized she was sobbing, unable to stop herself, with her face pressed into his furs.

She had no idea how long he let her cry.

Eventually she became aware that he had come to sit beside her. She could smell a kind of burning wood and she wrenched open her swollen eyes, the whole back side of her body alight. Perhaps that was why it took her so long to realize that he had taken hot ash from their fire and was working it into the grooves on his staff. Until he had blackened ten of them.

Then, without a word, his midnight gaze moving over her face, he held the staff out. Holding it toward her.

One dark brow arched high as she gazed at it, then at him.

"Thank you, Master," Eithne whispered, and she sounded duly chastened. It was the truth that she felt chastened, straight through.

And she kissed the staff, tasted ash on her lips, and told herself in the next moment that the taste was why the way he looked at her then made her shiver.

He set the staff aside. And as Eithne watched, still lying on her belly with her head turned toward him, he finally pulled himself out of his trousers.

She could feel her eyes grow wide. And more telling, could feel that shift inside her. For even though she ached, the mere sight of his huge male part made her breathless. It made her woman's flesh stir anew.

For she had forgotten how big he was. And more, how much she liked that.

"I expect you to find your pleasure, Eithne," he told her, his voice a deep rumble that seemed to move her bones, shifting them out of place. "And be quick about it."

"Ulfric…" she tried to say, but her mouth didn't seem to work.

For he was already moving. She could feel his hands on her, spreading her thighs wide as he knelt between them. And his hands were rough against the marks he'd put upon her, making her cry out as that white-hot fire ate at her anew.

But he did not hesitate. He hauled her toward him with an arm beneath her hips, then slammed his cock home.

And it was as if every part of her burst alight. All the pain, the tears, the impossible greedy hunger—

It all rushed through her, filling her up, too much to bear—

Ulfric pulled back only a little, just enough for her to note how truly massive he was as that thick, hard length found every part of her channel, and he was always just big enough that she wondered if she could truly take all of him—

But he gave her no choice. He simply slammed into her again, crashing all that power and glory deep inside her.

And then she heard that dark laugh of his all around her, and it was the end of her.

She simply…lost herself.

It was too huge, too wild, and this was what she'd called her curse. This was what she'd missed. She was nothing but the way he made her feel as he battered his way into her, and she was naught but an explosion, a reckoning, a wild reunion. She had no name, no thought, no goal—no purpose at all but to be used by him, to be part of him, to be this bright dance of flame and fever, forever.

This was what she'd dreamed of, all this time. This was what she'd craved.

She shook and she shook until he bellowed out his own pleasure at last. He slumped over her, setting all the marks he'd left on her alight all over again, as if they were gifts all along.

Eithne curled herself around the fire in her flesh, lost herself in the delight, and finally drifted off into sleep— pinned to his furs as if she had belonged here all along.

As if this was a homecoming.

Chapter Seven

It was as if she had never left him.

As if she had never dared take up that dagger or keep running when she'd heard him shout her name. As if the forests she'd wandered were naught but dreams, the life she'd carved out a story she might have heard sung once. In a hall in the dark of winter, while a storm raged on outside and all who could do so gathered close.

For too easily did she slip back into the life she had led as Ulfric's concubine.

She woke that first night to find herself in his furs, her hands freed from behind her back but once more tied in front of her. In the night, Ulfric liked to keep her wrists bound together and attached to the bed, and so she was not alarmed to wake and find herself so trussed. Unlike waking from her dreams of him all these long months, waking to find herself in this dark dwelling all in shadow save the crackle of the fire, with evidence of his power over her everywhere, did not make her… unnerved.

Or whatever that red heat had been all those mornings in the woods, prickling through her and leaving her sure she was made of naught but ash and shame.

Ulfric had moved her so that she lay mostly on her side and belly, and though she could feel too well all the marks he had left on her, she felt the strangest sense of peace. She almost smiled before her mind caught up with her. Before her gaze went to him as if she'd known where he was all along. While she'd walked across Northumbria. While she'd traveled.

For he sat by the hearth, stirring something in a small pot, and she knew what it was from the scent. She could smell the herbs as they perfumed the air. He pulled it off the fire to let it cool before he brought it over to the bed. His dark eyes met hers as he sat beside her and she felt his gaze like the kind of touch he'd used to give her at moments like this.

A moment later he demonstrated it, running his fingertips along her jaw, over her lips.

He did not say it, but she knew he was proud of her—of how she'd taken the staff—and it made her glad.

Here in the dark of night, she did not question herself for that feeling. She simply let herself feel it.

And then he set about smoothing the salve he'd made over the welts she could feel lining her bottom and thighs, stiffening now so there was a sharp tugging every time she moved. She watched him as he worked, could see the intent that changed his hard face. He was a warrior, battle-ready and ferocious, but here, in the quiet of the night, he was something else, too. It was not a softness, for there was nothing in him that was soft. It was almost as if he was some kind of artisan, yet instead of carving wood or chipping away at stone, he made his finest marks on her body.

Or maybe she only wished to tell herself these things because she needed them to be true. Because she needed to make this thing between them something more than what it was. His needs, her slavery.

"When did you last break your fast?" he asked her, his voice a low rumble.

It did not occur to her not to answer him.

"I had a crust of bread this morn," she murmured, though her eyes were still half-shut and the morning seemed as if it had happened to someone else. For surely she had always been here, lying warm and naked beneath his hands as he soothed the hurts he'd caused her and reminded her what it had always been like here. With him.

She had pretended her shame had been about her situation. About having become a slave through no fault of her own, with a master who, in the years she'd been with him, had never offered her even the hint of an opportunity to buy her way free as some did. But the true shame had been something else. It had been that beating heart of need between her legs. It had been the way her body was forever in a state of awareness, alertness. Ready for the faintest brush of his fingers or a sideways glance. Ready for all the terrible, wonderful things he did to her.

Ready and more willing.

When she had but dreamed of him, she had woken each day and reminded herself that she should have been furious. She should have dreamed of vengeance, not somehow finding him again for too many sinful other reasons. And already could she feel the change in her, as if the year and six months she had spent free were nothing. Not if the moment she returned into his clutches it was as if she had never left.

As if she'd never *wanted* to leave.

But tonight, Eithne told herself that she would wait to find that distressing. She would wait until she could sit up under her own power. For tonight, it was his hands that moved her. He pulled her up onto her knees and had her kneel there on the bed, her bottom stinging and painful as she cradled it with her own feet.

Ulfric came and sat beside her, feeding her bits of hard cheese and dried meats from his hands. He did not ask her when she'd eaten her fill. He fed her as it pleased him and stopped when he liked. When he thought she'd had enough.

And when he was satisfied, he came to his furs naked and pulled her to him. He held her next to him, his hands at her throat and his arm as her pillow. As he had always done, every night she had been with him.

Once more, Eithne slept so deep she was surprised she woke at all.

Eithne thought that he would keep her tied up here. Hidden away, as he had in Dublin. It had only been during the march to battle that she had seen the others, his kin and their people. And all the servants that came with them, most slaves like her, who had set up their camps along the way. Most slaves were accorded the scut work, always taking the most demeaning, the most menial jobs, and receiving little by way of care in return.

And there were other concubines about as well. Some who were free woman and had entered into their arrangements by their own choice. King Ragnall had a number of such women. All of them hoping to use their association with him to gain higher status for themselves or their clans, especially were they to give him sons he might claim as his heirs.

Eithne had always occupied strange space between those two extremes. For well did she know the difference between the marks on her body and the bruises she had sometimes seen on some of the other female slaves, who likely performed the same nightly duties she did but were also put to work all day. Ulfric had his own dwelling but ate most of his meals at his King's side, and therefore did not require that the woman he owned keep his home the way a wife might. She'd started to do some of those things before she'd left. Though she told herself it had been only because it was expedient, back when they had lived together in his tent and space was the primary concern.

Her first morning back in his clutches, he woke her the way he always had. She woke as his hands came around to grip her belly, tipping her even further onto her side. His cock notched itself into place so he could pull her back against him, so that the whole of his hard, sculpted chest was flush against her back and his hips nestled tight against her bottom as he thrust in, hard.

It had been another moment of revelation, of truth.

For he was all around her then, the hand at her belly and soon enough the whole of his arm to hold her in place. The implacable length of his cock inside her, waking up her body as he went, so that his first thrust was a spark, the second a flame, and the third of roaring fire that swept over her. As if she was like a hearth fire, simmering. Waiting. And he needed only that spark to bring her back to life.

Like all things Ulfric, it hurt as good as it felt. Every thrust ground his hips against her red, welted behind, until she was squirming to get away as much as she was thrusting her own bottom back for more. Both at once.

And there were things she didn't wish to know about herself buried here in the push and the pull, the tangle of it, the wild, mesmerizing heat she'd tried her best to escape.

He murmured dark words in her ear. Sinful commands, wicked compliments, and all of it pushed her further. All of it made it hotter. That red-hot blaze, that shame and remaking with every powerful thrust—

wrenching pleasure from her, taking it from her pain and making it his.

Ulfric reached around with his other hand to hold the proud peak of her woman's flesh between two rough fingers. Only that, the faintest hint of pressure, and she buckled into another bright red punch that left her shaking and sobbing.

His pleasure came soon after, rough and wild.

And for a long while they lay like that, tangled together.

Eithne had never known how it was that she was meant to pick up all the pieces of her soul that he left flung about, but she did.

She tried.

It was all so normal. It was as if she had but dreamed her seasons in the woods, the long, slow walk from Corbridge to Jorvik, with so many small villages and all those forests in between. It was as if Osthryth was the dream and this simply her life. Her bottom ever red. The welts from the staff had a particular bite today, but if it were not the staff it would be something else. He liked to make switches. He liked to see what different kinds of wood could do. For his was a twisted, wicked imagination, and she was his favorite plaything.

Once Ulfric arose and washed himself with the water he'd warmed by the fire, he unhooked her from the bed, unwound her hands, and let her do the same. He watched her as she took the length of wool, biting back the noises she wanted to make when she moved too quickly and made her welts sting. When she was finished, she hung up the cloth and he beckoned her to him with two fingers.

Eithne stood before him while he sat on the side of the bed and applied the salve to his own handiwork. When he was done, he turned her around to face him. His dark gaze swept over her face, and she knew too well that he saw everything. There was nowhere to hide from that midnight gaze.

What astonished her was how little she wanted to hide today, when that made no sense. He had taken her captive again. He had swept in and hauled her out of the market square. He had used his hand and his staff on her, and she should hate with all her might that the wickedness he practiced made his sins feel the way they did.

She had been so certain that having escaped him once, she would hate him forever.

Whatever he saw on her face amused him. She could see the light of it in his gaze. He bent his head to bid her sit in the chair near the hearth. And when she did, but gingerly, the corner of his mouth crooked up.

Because he quite liked his handiwork. He always had.

Ulfric handed her the drink of bitter herbs he made her each morn and settled there to watch her drink it. Eithne felt relieved that she felt the same resentment swell in her that she always had.

But today she had her voice. "There's no need for you to watch me so closely," she told him, watching him balefully over the top of her cup. "I have no desire whatsoever to tip these herbs out on the floor. That I shall have no child while a slave can only be a blessing."

Ulfric only watched her in that particular way he had that made everything in her still, while her cheeks heated up enough, she thought they must rival the red on her bottom.

"In this we are one," he said, and though he did not crack what passed for his smile, she could still see that he was amused. "But I do not watch you because I wish to see if you have the burning need to grow big with my child as some women do. I watch you because I like it."

"You like watching me choke down these bitter herbs?"

"I like watching what is mine do as she is told."

Eithne swallowed the last of her drink. "I suppose it is true that every man wishes himself a king, if only in his own furs."

Ulfric let the corner of his mouth rise further. Otherwise, he might as well have been made of stone. He sat there wearing but little, and she could see the gleam of his flesh in the firelight, the length of his beard, the glitter of his dark eyes.

It would have been better if he were not such an unquestionably handsome man. If he had been like the slavers in Dublin with their cracked lips, stained teeth, and vile odors, it would have been easy to hate him. More than easy.

That would have been simpler.

"That is so for many," he said at length, agreeing with her. She didn't know why that surprised her, but then, all of this was new. This *talking to Ulfric* made her feel as if the ground beneath her was not the ground at all. As if it might set her to rolling at any moment. "But not I. I have no wish to rule men."

"Then you are the only man I have ever met who can say such," she retorted, not bothering to hide her disbelief.

Perhaps because it felt better than asking herself why a simple conversation with this man made her feel as if she'd drunk too much ale.

"You have lived with me for years." His brow rose as he said that, but that was his only reference to the time she had lived without him. "Surely this cannot surprise you. I am satisfied with my life. With my sword and the oaths I have sworn to Ragnall. I do not have the same ambitions that others do."

"Your brother, you mean." Eithne remembered his brother Thorbrand better than she would like, and his cousin Leif, too. Leif had been the most engaging at first, always with a laugh, always ready for a joke and a song—though it had quickly become apparent that he was as deadly as the rest. Thorbrand, by contrast, had always been more watchful, more contained. A quieter kind of deadly. And when they had left Dublin for Northumbria and she'd seen life outside of Ulfric's dwelling, she'd seen that Thorbrand was indeed a leader of men and that the others looked to him.

Even Ulfric, who wore his own quiet ferocity like another fur.

"My brother does a favor for our King, far from here," Ulfric told her in that same intense manner of his. "He does his duty and so must we all."

He stood then, pulling a pot from the hearth that smelled rich, like game. Her mouth began to water. Especially when he brought out the end of a loaf of bread and set it out between them on the edge of the hearth.

"Eat," he told her. And when she hesitated, he handed her a wooden spoon and nodded toward the stew. Eithne did not dare disobey.

Especially when she was far too hungry, suddenly.

He pulled apart the bread in his big hands and popped a morsel in his mouth. "But it is not for me, the dream of sitting up over men in mead halls and stamping coins in my name. I swing a sword and loose my bow and care who is in my furs, not who graces the throne of lands I will never see. I like to drink in mead halls, not rule. I want a glorious death and honor to my name. Let me be a credit to my father's legend and a boon to my King, and I am happy." That dark gaze of his seemed to bite into her. "I am a simple man, Eithne. As I have told you."

"No one has ever accused you of such a thing," she replied softly.

His broad shoulders lifted, then fell. "And yet it is so. For what is given mortal men but a short time, if it please the gods. Time better spent in battle so that songs may be sung when we are gone."

"I thought men wanted sons to sing their songs when they were gone, to carry on their legacies," she said, nodding toward the cup of herbs she'd drained. "Or is it that you cannot bear the shame of having your sons born to a slave?"

The shame would be hers, Eithne knew, and much would depend on whether or not he chose to acknowledge that any child she bore was his. It was not required. She was not a free woman with a clan who might petition the King on her behalf.

"If the gods see fit to give me sons, so they shall," Ulfric replied with seeming unconcern. "But in the meantime, my little slave, I do not wish to share you. Not with a child. Not with my men. Not with anyone."

He did not demand that she thank him for that boon, and she almost said so—but stopped. For the look on his face was different, then. It was as if he had not known he meant to say such things.

As if this was not as easy for him as it seemed.

Ulfric stood then. Eithne waited for him to put his hands upon her again and teach her yet another version of that same lesson in wanting him despite herself. But instead, he moved across the hut and rifled around in a chest until he pulled out a fabric she recognized all too well.

It was the dress she had most often worn here. She'd come with the one she'd worn when she'd run from him, and had hidden beneath her ragged cloak. She had made another at his direction, kneeling naked before him as she'd sewed on those long evenings in his tent that first winter.

Eithne felt a great mix of things as he presented it to her, tossing it on the foot of the bed with a linen shift she had also left here. There was a certain pride in the dress, for she had liked greatly the fabric he had chosen for her. But, too, every stitch seemed infused with him. She could remember those nights in his tent while the snow fell outside. The way the quiet between them at times had been shot through with the true state of things.

All the time she spent upended over his lap, taking her nightly spankings. The low noises of approval he would make the back of his throat when she set her sewing aside and he drew her to him. Where she would stay on her knees before him, his fists wrapped in her hair and her hands behind her back as he guided her to him. As she took as much of him as she could in her mouth, doing her best to please him.

He always let her know when she did. Or did not.

It was as if she could see those nights again as she dressed now, in these clothes she'd thought she'd never see again. The shift she'd mended so many times it was more mending than original fabric, and soft as a whisper. The dress itself, a good wool that was far nicer than any she'd had in Dublin. The apron that she wore over it that she washed more than the rest, for it too often seemed to gather all the dirt around her.

She did her hair, braiding it in the manner she knew he liked. Not quite the coils of braids the married women wore and often covered. Not the free-flowing locks of innocent girls. She braided only the top and let the rest fall, because ever did Ulfric like to dig his hands into the length of it and guide her that way.

He grunted his approval when she was done.

Then he studied her. "I considered locking you in a cage," he told her in that mild way of his that made her heart begin to kick wildly within her chest. "But as tempting as that sounds, it would not give me the access to you I like to have."

"Also," she managed to say, though the shame was back again, a pulse between her legs, a loud singing in her ears. "I am not a dog."

His dark eyes gleamed. "I want you to think of that cage today. All of my people know well that I have spent all this time looking for you. They say I am bewitched. Enthralled."

"If that were so, the cage would be for you, would it not?"

And she regretted her tart words in the next moment, for his head tilted slightly to one side, the way it did when he was tallying up her offenses.

And there were always prices to be paid for offenses. For disrespect. For anything and everything he deemed necessary. Some rules she knew. She was to kneel before him when he entered, if they were alone and she were not tied in a way that prevented it. She was to thank him when he used implements like that staff. She was to keep her legs apart unless he put them together, she was to yield to him always, and sometimes, if he was in a mood, she was to fight off that terrible pleasure he pushed on her until he said otherwise. Other things he made up as they went along because it pleased him.

At the end of the day, that was what this was all about. Pleasing him.

What Eithne couldn't understand was why she wanted to. In those first years, she'd held on to her muteness because it was the only thing she could hold on to. And perhaps because she had that to point to, then. She'd been able to fall back on that and tell herself it was proof that she was not *truly* surrendering herself to him, and thus the ways in which she had tried to please him had felt less telling.

But now she had nothing to cling to. And so there was only her obedience, and what was she meant to do with that?

"Come," Ulfric said. "My King wishes to look upon this *huldra* I have finally reclaimed. Perhaps he will strike you down for running away from your master. If he does not, rejoice." But though his dark gaze made her belly flutter, she would not call that *rejoicing*. "For you and I can talk of cages all you wish."

Chapter Eight

But Eithne had no time to worry overmuch about cages, for Ulfric led her out into the light of day on this bit of road close to the castle, where his people were going about their busy lives. The women and servants were already deep into the day's work. There was laundry being hung while the weather was yet fine. One woman was directing her daughters in sorting through buckets of yellow flowers with bluish leaves—woad, Eithne thought. To make a blue dye they would use on their clothes. Women walked to and from the river with yoked buckets over their shoulders. They tended to the cows, called for their children, and brought chairs outside so that infirm elders could take in the soft breeze so close to Midsummer.

In a typical village, the men would be out working the fields, but this was not only Jorvik—home to markets and craftsmen and artisans alike—this particular sector was where Ragnall's fighting men were staying. So the men themselves were out in the road, too. Some looked to be coming back from hunting. Others had clearly gone fishing. Still others were covered in sweat and bruises, and were still trying to fight each other in the street—a part of the training men like Ulfric took part in daily, the better to serve their King should his enemies arise. And enemies always arose, as inevitable as winter following summer, no matter how sweet. This she knew.

Too many people stopped their labors to look at Eithne as she passed. Eithne could see that they all recognized her, if not by her face alone then because she walked with Ulfric and she could be no other but the concubine he had scoured the earth to find. But then, she realized that she recognized a great number of them, too. There were faces she knew looking back at her, and that sat in her strangely. It had been a long while since anyone had known her on sight. She had grown used to being skipped over, ignored. She had come to prefer the crone's life.

This is far better than beauty, Osthryth had told her the first time they had made Eithne look older than she was. *This is power. There is a reason men collect the one and yet wield the other.*

Eithne had no power, so she used what she did have. She stood taller. She held herself like a queen, not a slave, and little did she care if those who stared at her thought her a witch. Better that than what she really was—the girl who sobbed in Ulfric's arms, whether from pain or pleasure, she could not tell.

And she thought she understood why Ulfric was not

simply tying her up as he had before, as if she were no different from a cow he might own. He was likely trying to prove that he was not bewitched the way they claimed he was. He marched her through the streets toward the great hall, his hand heavy at the back of her neck. As they walked, she found herself searching the shadows for any hint of the face she wanted to see. The face she would recognize with joy, but Osthryth was nowhere to be seen.

She couldn't decide if that augured good or bad. She wanted, desperately, to see her friend so she could try to communicate, somehow, that she was well. Or well enough. So that the old woman would carry on as planned and worry about herself, not about Eithne.

Because Eithne kept being forced to confront the truth about her captivity. She was not free, there was no getting around that. But there were a great many ways to be a slave, and most of them were far worse.

There had always been slaves in Dublin, usually prisoners taken in one war or another, but it had never occurred to her that she ought to pay attention to their lot. For she was a free woman, the daughter of free men and women, and she had never lived in a time when the Northmen ruled. Slaves had been no concern of hers. She'd had her own work to do each day.

It had only been with Osthryth that she had paid more attention to the slaves they had encountered along their way. Not all were abused. Many, indeed, lived in the same dwellings as those they served and were fed and clothed. But almost without exception, they were all involved in various forms of manual labor.

All she had to do was take a little pain with her pleasure in a warrior's furs.

Woe is you, she mocked herself as she walked with Ulfric, past women whose eyes narrowed when they saw her, telling her they dreamed of taking her place. *Imagine if you were to tell these women with their jealous eyes what it is you suffer. They would claw their way into his bed to wear your chains.*

For they might all know that Ulfric had bought her in Dublin. It was true that many of them had known her as long as he had, for many were the wives and daughters of his kin and some had come with the men when they'd left Dublin. Others had come for the winters, settling down in the villages Ragnall and his men claimed to while away the coldest season.

But slave or not, it was well-known that Eithne was his concubine. And who among these women would not wish to share the furs of such a mighty warrior, so beloved of their King?

She found herself walking taller, keeping her expression serene as they moved. There was always that part of her that wanted to misbehave, to throw a fit, to try to shame this man before his people, but common sense always prevailed. For one, he would subdue any outbreak she might attempt, and well did she know it.

He would subdue it, and then he would exact a price for her outburst, and what was the point in that? She would be known as the slave who attempted to shame her master before his people, and none would look too kindly on it. They would cheer him on if he beat her for it.

Worse, such behavior might encourage him to sell her to someone else.

And it was good to remind herself that while her situation did not please her—and while there would always be that fire within her to escape this slavery, to return to Dublin, and to face her brother at last—it was a good thing to remember that there were many masters who took what they liked from their slaves, made them sleep in the dirt, treated them like dogs, and thought nothing of their comfort. What bruises they left behind they cared not. It was certain they did not soothe those marks with salve they made with their own hands.

Eithne was glad of the walk, because it gave her time to reacquaint herself with her position. And she needed that help and all the rest of the help she could muster, because Ulfric was taking her to see his King.

Ragnall, who had concubines aplenty and too many slaves to count, and who had always looked at her as if he, at least, remembered well that there was only one Ulfric. *You are replaceable*, the older man's hard gaze had seemed to say, though he had never spoken to her directly.

Nor should he have. For he was Ragnall, whose deeds were known and sung wherever men roamed. And who was Eithne but an interchangeable bedmate for one of the King's favorites?

She tried to hide her shiver as Ulfric walked her to the great hall, where the men who trained with their swords and their clubs called out his name. She tried to hide her disquiet as he led her inside. There were women working, as ever, sweeping up rushes as they hurried this way and that with piles of linens to launder. Or tended to the King's great hearth. Or scrubbed the long tables where men drank and sang and, some nights, bled.

Ulfric led her through the great hall where older men sat, their fighting days behind them, talking in low voices of battles past and future. Politics and power, as ever.

Then she saw the King's concubines, seated around the head of the table where Ragnall himself sat, too, looking as if he had spent a long morning on the training field. He saw Ulfric and nodded, beckoning him close.

Eithne studied the women, for that was less intimidating than sneaking a look at the formidable King himself. She wondered which one of them Ragnall had taken to his bed the night before. She'd played that game often when she'd last been among this company and was sure she could tell again today, by the smug look on one woman's face and the hard glances the others threw her way when the King was not looking.

But they all sat back when Ulfric brought Eithne

forth, and then it was naught but narrow eyes all round as they looked her up and down. No doubt they thought her skinny, but Eithne took some pride in the fact she was not weak or disfigured. Yet.

"Do you bring this slave before me so I might mete out punishment for her crimes?" Ragnall boomed.

He had always terrified her, this Northman King. She had heard tales of this man and his kinsman, the terrible Sitric who even now sat over Dublin, long before she had ever encountered either one of them. Back when Northmen had been scary stories told around the fire to scare the children into behaving.

Back before she'd come to understand that monsters were all too real.

Ragnall was an older man, and older now than the last time she had seen him, but there was nothing weak about him. He had gone gray, yet it was clear he could still swing his sword. And the women who would have vied for his bed in any case, because he was King, always whispered about him as if he were a much younger man. Ragnall, they said, had the stamina of ten men and never left a woman unsatisfied.

These were the sorts of conversations she would have longed to hear when she had still been a maid in Dublin. The practical things women knew of men, the frank manner in which they discussed them at the slightest provocation, and why not, when men were everywhere and needed so much handling—it seemed such a waste to Eithne that the innocent were kept out of the places where such things were discussed. That it was deemed too much for their tender ears.

When it was the innocent who needed to know the most, by her reckoning. It was the innocent who found a sisterhood after the fact, instead of mentors beforehand.

It was all backward, to her way of thinking.

Not that anyone had asked. Certainly not the King's concubines, all of them free women and a great deal higher in rank than the slave of one of the King's men. Even if that man was Ulfric.

For a new game, because it was better than attempting to meet Ragnall's cold glare, Eithne asked herself which of these women she thought had warmed Ulfric's furs in her absence—

But it turned out, she had no stomach for it. If anything, the very notion made hers go sour.

"I told you I would find her, and so I have," Ulfric was saying. "Just as I told you last night."

"Slaves risk death when they run," Ragnall rumbled. "It is near certain when they take up arms against their masters. What have you to say for yourself, girl? Is there some reason I should stay my hand, or order your master to let you live?"

She did not dare turn around to try to look for help from Ulfric, standing there like a cold mountain behind her.

Her heart beat so loud, so hard, it hurt.

In truth, she did not think that Ulfric would have brought her here if he thought Ragnall would smite her down where she stood. But that was the thing with kings. They could do as they liked. And usually did.

"If you will forgive me, sire," she managed to say, her head bowed. "If you will… What person alive today does not dream of freedom, whatever it means to them? And who, having lost it, would not seize it if they could? Even a lowly girl like me."

She could see only her own feet and her hands, clutched before her. The hall was not silent, and the noise from within her was near deafening. But she had no trouble feeling the sort of long, heavy look that the King and Ulfric exchanged.

Even if she had no idea what it meant.

Once again, she fought to keep her shiver hidden, even though she knew that Ulfric could likely feel it. His hand still gripped her neck.

"If Ulfric wished to stone you right here in my hall, I would not prevent him," Ragnall told her after some while, and Eithne could hear the truth in his voice. She knew he meant that, and this time, could not hide the fearful shudder that moved through her. "If you were my property, I would flog you raw. I might yet, for searching for you has weighed heavily on my man's mind this last year. Were he any other, it might have prevented him from serving me well. This I cannot abide."

"No… No, sire," she whispered.

"Look at me," the King bade her.

And Eithne had no choice but to obey him. She lifted her head and met his gaze as best she could. He lounged there in his chair, his face stern, and she did not need the warning grip at her neck to know that this was no time to test the edge of her tongue. For there were men, even mighty ones like Ulfric, and then again there were kings.

Men work the land, Osthryth liked to say. *Kings make it into kingdoms.*

"I will not have you the talk of my court," Ragnall told her, his voice even harder than his gaze, a terrible steel. "I will not have the exploits of a slave the only songs sung or story told. Do you understand me?"

She could only nod, aware that she was holding her breath but unable to do anything about that.

Ragnall kept his gaze trained on her. "It would behoove you to make certain I have no reason to think of you again. For I do not wish to think of any slaves but my own. If I were you, girl, I would learn the value of knowing your place."

Eithne only bowed her head, wishing she could make herself small. And knowing she no more wished for his notice than she wished to become a king herself.

Ulfric moved her then, his hand at her nape, and bid her sit on one of the benches farther down the table. She did so happily. Gratefully. And as he and Ragnall spoke in low voices, she became dimly aware that the other women had not gone far, and even now murmured about her.

She lifted her head and found them all staring at her, each of them haughty in their own way.

"Is it true?" asked Gudrun. She had been big with child when last Eithne had been at court and she wondered, idly, if the baby lived. Gudrun had always had an air of smugness about her, but it seemed even greater than she recalled, so she assumed the woman had indeed given the King a child. It would make sense, then, that she was the first to speak directly to the slave Ragnall had just chastised. "Did you disguise yourself? As a beggar woman?"

And the King had bade her keep her counsel and fade away. But if a favored concubine of his reported that she had failed to respond when asked directly, was that not its own provocation? And what trouble would that bring?

Eithne had never expected that she would have to deal with such intrigue. She had expected to live her whole life as most did, in the same place where she'd been born. If all had gone as planned, her parents would have lived. She would have been long married by now, with babies of her own. She might even have died in childbirth, like so many others, and unlike these men who spent their lives in halls like this, no songs would be sung for a simple life lost in Dublin. No stories were ever told of a quiet, unremarkable life that had carried along as it should.

Today, that sounded to her like a blessing.

For she was a simple Irish girl having to play courtly games in the hall of the Northman King, and she liked it little. It made the simplicity of Ulfric's demands, with only one possible way to obey them, all the more appealing.

"Not a beggar woman, my lady," she replied, keeping her eyes politely averted. "The old woman took me in and taught me her ways. She is a healer in the old style, that is all."

"They say she is a witch." Gudrun laughed heartily. "But I say she is nothing so interesting as that. Just another *frilla* cluttering up the streets and looking for handouts."

Eithne thought it was a bit rich to use that word to call Osthryth a whore when it was also the word used for concubines, but she did not say so. She felt nothing but weary as the other woman murmured sounds of assent, or looked at each other without quite pulling faces, showing her where the battle lines were drawn among the King's women.

It made her wish she was a man. If she was, she could stand on the battlefield and know that the enemy approached from one direction. That they could clash swords, head-on and direct.

Not these quiet wars that women waged, soft scents and sweet smiles, where none were ever the victor and all lost.

She longed for the woods again. For the wind in her hair, the stars for her walls. With only the trees for companions, some days.

Instead, she tried to make herself look smaller than she was. For surely if she was small enough, pathetic enough, these women who dreamed of wielding the King's power would dismiss her as unworthy of their exalted attention.

"I'm nothing but a slave, my lady," she murmured. "I'm sure you have the right of it."

Then again, maybe it was a good thing that Ulfric had brought her here. Because layered somewhere beneath her apprehension was a little spark of hatred. For these women. For her position. For the fact she dared not speak her mind as she would have done if she were free.

She clung to it.

Her meekness must have been deemed sufficient, for the women seemed ever bored and turned back to sniping amongst themselves. Soon enough they wandered off, but Eithne stayed where she was. And as Ragnall and Ulfric continued talking, still in voices none could overhear, she gradually became aware of the other women again.

Not the treasured concubines and their borrowed glory. But the women like her, simple and ordinary, who were here to clean the hall, do their part, and live their lives as untouched by the affairs of kings and warriors as if they were not standing in the same halls as Ragnall. As if they were villagers in one of the many small, forgotten places Eithne had found with Osthryth, where kings were only in songs sung around the fire when the hour grew late.

She found herself watching one girl who looked to be about her same age, also a slave. Eithne could tell by her rough-sewn dress. She was scrubbing the tables of the stickiness from a long night of men and their ale, songs, and feasting. But her eyes kept cutting to Eithne, and finally, she glanced around the hall.

When she looked back, she drew a line across her face, like Ulfric's scar.

And then smiled.

Then she hurried back to her tasks before anyone else could take notice.

Eithne looked down at her lap, hiding her own smile.

And it was only then that it occurred to her that Ulfric did not have her secured. There were no ropes tying her to this table. His hand was not upon her.

She lifted her gaze, but cautiously, and looked around the hall. Ulfric stood yet with Ragnall at one end of the table. The concubines chattered amongst themselves. The lower women still bustled about, performing their usual chores. There were only a few men, and none near.

Did she dare?

Everything in Eithne roared at her to rise, to run—

But she thought it through. This was not like last time. They were not on a battlefield, for one thing. The forests were some distance from this hall. In the meanwhile, there was nothing to slow Ulfric down. He would be on her fast, and there would be nothing to keep Ragnall from making good on his threat to flog her. Or stone her. Or simply kill her.

And even were she to somehow make it out of the hall, what then? This part of Jorvik was thick with Ulfric's kin and comrades. If the walk here had taught her anything, it was that she was known to all—and Ulfric even more so.

Her heart beat hard, as if she'd already leaped to her feet and started running.

She had to clench her hands hard in her lap, until she felt the pinch of it. The pain was better. It helped. She stared down at her stinging fingers until her gaze grew blurry, and did not let go until she were calm.

When she raised her head again, Ulfric was coming toward her.

And for a moment, it was as if everything spun around. For she sat in a hall, at a bench at a long table, as she had done no few times in her youth. She was dressed not as a woman three times her age, hidden away in rags and scraps and dirt. The dress she'd made was pretty, and it suited her well enough. It was a bit large on her today, that was all. Even her hair was washed and braided, when it had been a matted mess of ash for so long.

She could not remember the last time she'd felt so… regular.

Just a girl in a hall, like the girl she might have been had Feargal not betrayed her. A girl in a hall as a handsome warrior drew near.

Eithne felt that pulse in her kick in again, even harder than before.

And she had the strangest, most dizzying thought, then. The most dangerous thought yet.

What if that was truly who they were? What if she was free and found herself in the hall of a king, only to see such a mighty, powerful man walk toward her like this? Even if she didn't know the way this man could tempt her, tease her, and take her to places she dared not name?

Ulfric's gaze was dark, yet lit from within as ever. The way he focused on her, it was as if the hall, his King, and even the great sprawl of Jorvik fell away.

She felt her heart swell, as if she really was that girl. As if this was her *choice*.

And even as it did, a kind of grief seized her.

For she was not free. She had not chosen him, and could not.

And want him though she might, long for him though she did, however shamefully—there was no changing who they were.

There was no pretending.

But for that one, treacherous moment, her traitorous heart tried. To pretend. To wonder.

To ask herself, *what if?*

He stopped before her and she rose, taking her cues from his gaze, as ever. And despite that fluttering, terrible longing she wished she'd never let herself feel, she felt something else when he slid his hand to her neck again, to hold her there. His palm was a jolt of heat against her bare skin. She wanted to look around wildly, to see who watched them. For surely they could see that there was something sinful about his touch. About *him*. Surely someone would find this scandalous.

But as ever, she could see only Ulfric. And Eithne could not bring herself to look away from the face that had haunted her for so long. Eyes so dark she could stare at them forever. The bold lines of his cheeks and his jaw, evident even beneath his beard. His braids, bound back today, marked him the unflinching, relentless Northman he was in all things.

And well did she know it.

"Do you feel duly chastened?" he asked, mildly enough. "Have you learned your place?"

And once again, that terrible wish rolled through her, making her very legs beneath her feel unsteady. *What if?*

What if her brother had married her to this man? What if they had clashed eyes across the Dublin market and he had offered for her? What if he had married her and only then taught her all of these things that bound them even now...but had allowed her the option to say no?

Even if she never used it?

In that moment, Eithne understood something she never had before. Too focused had she been on her circumstances, and rightly so. For never had she asked herself this.

And she understood why. Because it was nothing less than shattering.

Because had he only asked, had he courted her, had

he allowed her, as a free woman, to choose—she would have chosen this. Him. Eithne might even have told herself it was a practical decision. It was what women did, after all. Ever came the conquerors, to pillage and crush, and it was the smart woman who made herself one of them.

Not spoils of war, then, but *safe*.

She knew in her bones that was precisely what she would have done with Ulfric, had she been given the opportunity to choose him.

But she had not.

She could not.

Eithne felt the way his gaze moved over her then. That faint crease appeared between his brows, and that intensity seemed to hum in him, telling her how closely he did pay attention to her. How easily he read her.

And the strangest thing yet was how desperately she longed to tell him all of the things that rolled about inside her. How urgently she wanted to share her *what if*—so much so that it seemed to hover there on the tip of her tongue—

But instead, she blew out a breath and strove to steady herself before him. And all she whispered was the only thing she could. "Yes, Master. I know my place."

Chapter Nine

Midsummer came, and with it, the usual celebrations.

And though Ulfric took his errant concubine out because it was that or risk more talk of enchantments, he was always greedy to get her home again.

Where he could shut the heavy door, strip away her clothes, and glut himself on her exquisite surrender.

Because he still couldn't believe that he had found her again. That she was here, where she belonged. That she was not a dream come to torture him until he woke, in a fury and all alone.

Each night she chose another ten strikes of the staff, and so it was that each night he concocted a variety of ways to make them both happy with how and where he delivered them. Her happiness was more complicated, to be certain.

But Ulfric knew but few things in this life for certain: that the gods would do as they wished and that fate played no favorites. That he would serve his King and fight with honor until he fell, which could as easily be tomorrow as a dozen years hence, when he was gray and withered. And that it was only in the depths of her deepest surrender that his Eithne was most herself.

One night, he had delivered her ten strokes after securing her to one of the wooden posts that kept the little house's thatched roof high. And when all ten marks gleamed fresh on her flesh, she hung limp and let out that low humming sound she made that told him she was far away inside herself. He had taken her that way. From behind, slow and intense, gripping her hips and holding her up at an angle so she bore the weight of her body on her bound hands, suspended between the post and his cock.

And when he'd had her sobbing out his name like an oath, he, too, threw himself over that edge, losing himself in that tight, sweet grip.

There was none like Eithne. There never would be. Well did he know this.

Ulfric loosed her wrists, then took his time attending to her welts by the fire and cleaning her of her own honey and his spend. There was a peace in this, he found himself thinking when he was done and she knelt next to his chair, resting her head on his leg with her eyes closed. He toyed with her hair in the firelight, admired the soft curve of her cheek, and felt the strangest sensation creep over him.

It was peace, he was sure of it, though it were like no peace he had ever known.

For Ulfric had always disdained these times between

battles and had only ever suffered through them. He had never wished to settle. His two oldest brothers had died well in battle. His father had died as he had attempted to hold off the Irish Kings, his mother had died protecting her home in the same fight. How could Ulfric wish for anything different?

He didn't. He hadn't.

Ulfric had followed Ragnall ever since they had been thrown out of Dublin. And though Ulfric had been no more than a callow lad of fourteen when he'd left, he had grown into a man with every clash of steel he had dealt and fought off. He had fought in Ragnall's name from the Isle of Man to this cold island, and back again along the Irish coast. The only peace they had ever known was in the march to a new fight, and that was how he liked it.

It had never occurred to him until now that there was a different kind of peace. That it could be inside him, not imposed from without. That it could have nothing to do with the whims of his King, the cruelties of fate, or the bitter wrangling over these contested lands that never seemed to end.

Tonight, he wondered idly if it could be no more than this. Simplicity. His woman, marked from his own hands, yet still taking her rest like this. As if she took as much comfort from him as she did reel in the suffering they both craved.

He felt something in him mend itself together like a woman's stitching, though he would have sworn no part of him lay broken or needed thread and needle to repair. Still, it was as if a fragile sort of cloth stretched between them and grew with each breath. With every pattern he drew over her skin or traced over the sweet shell of her ear.

Ulfric found he liked it.

"You miss your brother," she murmured, almost as if she spoke to the hearth fire.

His hands stilled. Earlier today, he and Leif had toasted far off Thorbrand and the great deed of honor he had undertaken for their King. Then they had fought each other as they did each morn as a training exercise and laughed, for they knew that were Thorbrand still among their number, he would have found himself unable to keep from assuming command.

This eve, Ulfric had taken his woman to Ragnall's hall for the evening meal. Songs had been sung and cups overfull had been lifted. Thorbrand's name had rung out. When he did not return before the coming winter, Ulfric knew some would say he had perished. For most only knew that he had taken a wife and then gone with some others to scout land to the west of Ireland. If he were another man, they would whisper that he merely chose not to return, for many men did settle in far-off places and forget their way home. There were laws to release wives from such husbands, for ever did a man seek land and though people might tut, secretly none could blame them. For who was not seduced by the notion of land to call their own?

Particularly this land, where a man could settle free and clear of the barbarous clans that had battled here for so long. And where a man could choose who he was and make himself new, if he desired.

Ulfric himself had seen this land the *skalds* called Snæland the previous summer, when he and his brother and cousin had sailed to Ísland and back, to ensure that Thorbrand could take up this mission when the time came. Even though it was little better than an exile, and all three of them had known it well.

But Thorbrand had been loyal. Was loyal still, no doubt. And though he had never said how little he had wanted the task assigned to him, Ulfric had known it. For what man wanted to be banished from battles and sent off to become a farmer, all in the hopes that his woman could be used as leverage at some future date?

Particularly when so many would sing of him and think him dead and gone.

Still, it would be better that he was thought dead than that any might put together the disappearance of the lady of Mercia's only daughter and one of Ragnall's favorite man.

Yet tonight, still, his brother was not yet thought dead, and so Ulfric had sung of him and the honor his brother had long brought to the family name.

For they were all of them descendants of Ivar the Boneless, that great hero of the clan who had carved his name in blood across these cold isles. Long would they all sing his songs. And tell many tales of his brave deeds. All of them who yet lived would stand in halls bright with mead and flatter themselves that they, too, might find their way into these sung histories, one brave deed of time.

Had Eithne asked him of his brother's great deeds, Ulfric could have sung them. And would have, with pleasure.

But she had not asked him such a thing. She had spoken instead of *missing* his brother, and Ulfric had let down his guard without realizing it, clearly. It was that strange and not entirely comfortable peace moving in him the way it did this day. It was making him imagine he were a different kind of man.

In this moment, he felt like that man. Not himself at all.

"Thorbrand is but one winter my elder," he told her, his gaze yet on the picture she made, her head nestled on his thigh. "We have been always in each other's company." He found himself scowling toward the fire, then. "I know where he is and what he does there. He serves our King with every breath, and there can be no greater glory."

He felt her smile, because her jaw moved beneath his hand. He did not need to look down to see it, though he did. Because her smile…did something to him. He could not explain it.

But it, too, made him feel like a different kind of man.

"You could also have said, *Yes, Eithne,*" she teased him. *"I miss him."*

Ulfric found his scowl was no more. And that he, too, smiled. Not merely a lift at the corner of his mouth, when he would have said that was all he had to offer. Though he was sure he would prefer the sharp edge of the blade rather than admitting such.

"We will meet again, my brother and I," he said with great certainty. "If not in this life, then we will drink deep in the halls of Valhalla."

She burrowed her face into his thigh. Her hands were free for the moment, so she wrapped them around his leg and held on to him that way. And he took a pleasure in that he could not have described. It made his heart pound as if he were at a dead run, so deep was it. So unexpected.

So impossible without her.

"My sister was the same for me," Eithne murmured into the quiet between them, and it was an oddity, he thought, that he could hear her perfectly when she was speaking so softly. When surely his own blood in his ears should have drowned her out. "We were both born in the same year. We grew up almost as one."

Ulfric wanted to ask, *Did your brother sell her, too?* Yet something kept him from it. She had not spoken of her family since he'd found her in Jorvik, save that very first day. And then only to mention her brother. He had known her brother had sold her to the slavers. He remembered that much from Dublin. But as for the rest of her family, she had been playing mute in those first years she'd been with him and thus had told him nothing.

He wanted to know, but for some reason, he did not wish to remind her that she was his slave in this moment.

It was the strangest urge within him. He could not understand it.

Ulfric found himself rubbing at his own chest and frowned down at his hand.

"Where is she now?" he asked her instead. She sighed, but slightly, and yet he thought her grip on him tightened.

"She took ill three winters before you Northmen came." He wanted to say, *Before we came back, for Dublin was ours first*, but did not. And was glad he had not, because she kept going. "They all died. My parents. The sister I mentioned, Fainche. And all the little ones besides. It was a fever that took too many, not only my family. One day they were all well. Then one began to cough, and soon after all the rest. They were gone before the next moon."

He had a stray memory then, one he almost never revisited. The terrible day he and Thorbrand had found their mother's body, another casualty of the Irish Kings' bloody rampage. Of his father's funeral soon after, the burning ship in Dublin's harbor one of his last memories of the only home he had known until then.

He had forgotten those things in all the battles since.

All the places he had lived. All the camps he had called home, for as long as the battle raged.

Or he had tried to forget them, more like.

"It is easier, perhaps, when they are taken by an enemy," he found himself saying, as if he wished to comfort her with his words in the same way he did each night with the salve he made with the same hands that caused her wounds. The words sat heavily on his tongue, but he did not swallow them back. "You cannot fight fever. You cannot take revenge on its sons."

"If I could have done so, I would do it still," Eithne said, her voice as fierce as it had been when he'd come upon her in that alley. "Fainche was the best of us. She was so bright, so merry. She wanted naught but to help every person she saw, and had she but one crust only she would break it into pieces and feed others before herself." She was quiet a moment, though Ulfric imagined he could feel her agitation in the way she gripped him. In the softness that no more suffused her. "I would have told you that I could not survive her loss."

He played with her hair, curling a strand of it around and around one finger. "And yet you live."

"And so we must," Eithne said, her voice low. "Far beyond what seems possible."

Ulfric reached down for her then, shifting her around so she faced him. Because he wanted to see her face. He needed it, just then. He brushed his thumbs beneath her eyes, looking for wetness, yet found none.

Still, there was a darkness in her gaze he didn't like.

A heaviness about her where before there had been only their particular joy.

He wanted more of it.

And he wanted so much of it that it could never turn heavy again, no matter what ghosts might rise.

He had been so certain he wanted her back because he'd wanted to punish her for leaving, but that was a lie. He had wanted this, though he could not have known to dream of it. These quiet moments with her that made all the battles he fought seem worth it, in and out of his furs.

She made his heart feel like it belonged to her, not him.

"There is no bartering with the Fates," he told her then, but not as harshly as he should have done. "You might as well try to row against the wind, for they will do as they like. What has happened and what will happen have already been decided."

"And well do I know it," she replied, but still there was that darkness in her.

He tried to remember that she was but a Christian. "There is no honor in succumbing to fate, little slave, as if it is a rock crushing you into the earth. It is how you meet your fate that matters. It is all that matters."

Something in the vicinity of his chest shifted at that, yet he ignored it. And he judged that there was sufficient spark in her gaze then, green and bright. He shifted in his chair, and then patted his knee.

He didn't have to tell her what to do. She already

knew. And as he watched, the temper she was usually wise enough to hide from him flashed over her face.

"Do you ever ask yourself what it is that went wrong, Ulfric?" she asked him softly, deliberately. Recklessly. "What is that curdled within your soul to make you like this?"

He felt that edgy, deliciously cruel twist in the corner of his mouth. He watched as her eyes widened and knew she saw it for what it was. A warning she did not intend to heed.

Too easily could he read the foolhardy glitter in her gaze. And he knew as well as she did that she did this willfully.

He knew what she wanted.

Because he knew, as she did, that when their particular fire rose so high between them, they both craved the burn of it. That impossible burn, that unforgettable release.

They were two halves of the same whole. Well did he know it. But never more than at moments like this.

"The same thing that must be wrong with you." His voice was quiet, but he knew well his gaze was not. "Can you name it, little slave?"

Her gaze was like a dagger. Like the one she'd once used to cut him that he wore on his belt. "Too many deaths, but who cannot say the same in these dark times?" She cocked her head slightly to one side, not even attempting to strip the insolence from her movements. "Though I have not swung a sword to add pain and death to others' burdens. I doubt you can say the same."

"I have no wish to say such," Ulfric retorted. "Look around, Eithne. This world is treacherous. Better to be brave and strong than to cower. To let others decide your fate rather than test your strength."

"Do you think this is strength?" she asked, in that sharp tone that matched a certain look she'd used to give him that he had told her on too many occasions to count already that he could not abide. Which only made her use it more, at times like this. Her voice made it worse. Or better, to his mind. "The things you do to a woman who cannot resist you. By law."

"Little slave," he said, his voice rich, for well did he enjoy this. He could feel his cock, hard and ready. "This is a dangerous game you play. You must not wish to sit down again this summer."

"My mistake," she said coolly, though he could see the hot flush of hunger sweep over her, making even her breasts red. "I did not realize that it mattered what I wished."

Ulfric laughed at that. Then he took her by the neck and lifted her up from her knees delighting in the way she flushed an even deeper red, because he knew well that she loved the feel of his hand at her throat thus. He didn't choke her. He only held her.

She loved the way he held her thus and he knew it, though she did not have to tell him. It was the way her eyes glazed over with heat. It was in the way her woman's flesh dampened with need. It was written all over her, like so many runes carved into her flesh and her movements and the heat of her skin. So he held her there for a moment. Then used his other hand to lay her out over his lap.

And to his great joy, she fought.

She writhed against him, as if struggling to escape, and he laughed again. For there were nights when what he craved was her obedience. Her easy and total surrender.

But there were other nights, like this. When what both of them needed was to face their truest selves. She needed to be conquered. And he needed to conquer her.

This was the truth of him, of her. This dance of theirs, where both of them could be whole. Only like this.

Only together.

Because, for both of them, peace—no matter how deep, or how unexpectedly sweet—was only won on the battlefield.

This was theirs, where both of them were the victors, as long as they both fought.

And so they did.

Tonight, he spanked her hard and long. He spanked her until she sobbed, and the same storm washed through him, washing him clean. Then he hauled her up and spread her legs wide over his lap, taking her at a thunderous clip. One hand sank into her hair, pulling her head back to offer him the bounty of her neck, her breasts. His other arm anchored her hips where he wanted them. She went from sobbing in one way into sobbing in another, but she was still mad at him. So when he let loose her hair and she began to fall apart around him, she leaned forward as if it were their days of old, and bit him.

Hard.

Because both of them could do as they wished, here. No matter what.

Only with each other, where pain and pleasure tangled together, making them something far greater than they were alone. One battle at a time.

Ulfric roared out his pleasure as he poured himself deep within her.

And then he pulled her off him, threw her back over his lap, and spanked her more.

He kept on and on, through the threats, through the begging, until a new kind of sobbing took her over.

Only then did he stop and gather her to him. And he held her there in his lap as she rested her face in the crook of his neck, then sobbed until she was still. One hand curled up over his heart, for she liked to feel it beat.

For you, he thought. *Always for you.*

He carried her to the bed and curled himself around her, holding her there in the usual way until she fell asleep.

Ulfric held her long after, late into the night, and

told himself that it was still for her comfort when he knew better.

And he remembered too well what had happened the last time he had trusted a night like this. When he had believed that the spark between them erased everything else, that the way he knew her was what mattered, not how they had come to be here together.

It was so tempting to forget it. It was so tempting to think that everything had changed. That they had found, somehow—despite who they were and where they came from—their own sanctuary with each other.

She had fooled him once already. On a night too much like this one, he had imagined that what had passed between them was so profound that there was no further need to tie her to the bed. That what tied them together needed no ropes.

So he had woken to find her taking advantage of the ropes to tie him to the bed instead. She'd been working on his second hand and when he'd felt it as he'd woken, she'd cut him with his own blade. It was only after he'd freed himself of the knots she'd tied in the rope that held him that he'd staggered out to find her gone. And worse, that the battle he was there to fight, having nothing to do with his concubine, needed his attention.

He'd pretended that it was his pride that had been cut the worst that day, no matter the gash on his face.

The truth of it was something he liked to admit far less often, even to himself.

There was something sacred in these exchanges be-

'tween them. He knew it well. He knew she did, too. He knew that others did not stitch together sex and pain, control and surrender, in the way he did. The way she longed for, too. He knew precisely how rare it was to find a woman who met his every need, and so completely.

So fully it had been as if she'd taken more than a dagger from him. It was as if she had stolen a limb.

That she was his slave, then and now, seemed a gift from the gods, for how else would he have found her?

She made him dream of things he had never imagined for himself. A happy dwelling, filled with warmth and laughter. A smile on her pretty face, babies at her breast—when he was bred to be naught but a warrior, bound for Valhalla.

Eithne made him wonder if there were other, deeper joys than dying for his King on a blood-soaked field.

And of all the things in this life that he could not forgive, it was this that smarted most. That he had bared himself to her, left himself defenseless before her. He, who had never let another close since he was a lad. And she had stabbed him. With his own knife.

When he might make her cry, from pain and pleasure alike, but he ever and always protected her.

Ulfric knew, better than he liked, that it was not the mark she'd left upon him that bothered him still. It was that he had trusted her, foolishly. And she had used that trust against him.

He, who trusted nothing save his own strength, his own sword.

Thus tonight, though he once again felt that current between them—that understanding, that sacred space—he pulled back and made sure she was securely tied before he allowed himself to fall asleep beside her.

He blamed her for that, too.

And took it out on her tender backside for days afterward, with singular intent, though he did not tell her why.

The woman did not need any further weapons to use against him.

It came as something of a relief when Ragnall summoned him one afternoon, later into the summer, to tell him that Sitric had finally sent his messenger.

And more, that the time had come at last for Ulfric to get back to what he did best.

Chapter Ten

"Dublin?"

Eithne repeated the word as if she did not know it. As if it were some unfathomable bit of Norse tossed into the usual Irish they spoke to each other. As if she had never heard the name of her own home.

And it was true she stared at Ulfric without comprehension, even though, deep inside, something in her stirred to life.

Not that red shame she had come to understand was something far more complicated than fury, or longing— or shame, for that matter. This was something far darker.

And it had Feargal's name stamped all over it.

"Surely this is what you want," Ulfric said, and she instantly prickled to attention at the tone of his voice. Her gaze flew to his. She went still as she tried her best to guess his thoughts. His mood. What it might mean—for her.

He'd been summoned to see the King as he often was. Eithne had remained behind, wearing his favorite invention. He'd made for her a harness of rope that wound tight around her rib cage, emphasizing her breasts beneath her dress and biting in tight at her waist. She had complained throughout the process of his tying her into it with wicked little knots and loops, and had received a switching for trouble. And yet when he'd left her here, the harness connected to one of his longer ropes, she found she liked it.

It was difficult to make her way about the small dwelling with the long rope forever at risk of dragging in the hearth and causing a fire that would possibly kill her, but would certainly humiliate her should the neighbors see how Ulfric's concubine was kept docile. Like a horse.

Yet when she had complained about that, too, Ulfric had archly suggested that if she sounded so trembling and afraid of a rope, he could truss her up from head to toe. And leave her tied up like that, with a gag in her mouth and no possibility of setting any accidental fires to his things, until he was moved to return.

He had suggested such in so silky a tone that she knew he was likely to take a trip off to the coast or into the forests, to leave her lying like that as long as possible.

She had wiped her face clear of any expression he could categorize as *sulky*. And when he had left to attend to Ragnall, she'd stayed where she was, kneeling next to his chair. She had tested the limits of her breath against the rope wrapped tight around her, pressing her fingers into the knots.

It was as if he was there, holding her fast. As if his brawny arm was pressed tight against her, holding her down.

Just the way she liked it.

And she could admit, once she was alone, that she liked the rope harness far better than she cared to admit.

He had left in her favorite sort of mood. That light in his gaze and the promise of a delicious retribution in the curve of his mouth. As the days passed, he had slowly allowed her to return to her former duties for him. He locked his weapons away in the chest he kept at the foot of his bed, but she could set herself to mending his garments. She could do the washing. One of her major duties was keeping the water warm enough so that it could be heated easily when he returned, so he might have the daily bath he insisted upon.

And he allowed no other in the place where he slept, so she also cleaned the small house. She aired out the rushes. She tended to his furs, hanging them for air and cleaning them with his sweet-smelling soap. She did all the tasks she had learned to do at her mother's side. She and Fainche, as the oldest girls, had told each other grand stories as they'd worked. Of who their husbands would be, come the day. Of how many babies they would raise. It made her smile to think of her sister now, forever fourteen summers, and ever the sweet girl she had been then.

Eithne didn't know why she had told him about Fainche but she was glad she had, for now it was as if her sister was with her yet again. A memory grown sweet with time, for what she recalled now was Fainche's life, not her death.

And yet all of that fled her mind as she studied Ulfric's face now.

He looked...closed off.

In a way he had not been for some while.

She was too wrapped up in him these days. It was as if she could feel his moods deep inside. And too often between her legs, like now, for the more forbidding and even cruel he looked, the more she wanted him.

Pay attention, she snapped at herself.

"What I want?" she asked, echoing what he had said. "I don't follow you, I fear. At what point has what I want tipped the scales?"

He studied her as he moved farther into the room, and he didn't look as he had when he'd left. There had been a playfulness then that was missing now, but her body exulted in it all the same. Her nipples went tight and hot. Her skin seemed to pull tight. And between her legs, she was slippery and ready, as ever.

Almost as if the more dangerous he was, the more she wanted him.

Or maybe the real truth was that she always wanted him. However he came to her, whatever tricks he intended to pull and did, she wanted him. More and more, as if her hunger for him were truly insatiable.

And she could no longer tell if it were grief or longing, resignation, or, worst of all, love.

It was all of those things at once, she feared. It was all braided in and around itself, this monstrous wanting. This impossible man. These things they did.

The rope hugged her tight and she wished it were tighter still.

"We leave at first light," he told her gruffly.

Eithne swallowed and shifted the pair of his trousers that she'd been mending off her lap. "How long does it take?" she asked, though it seemed the very last thing that ought to occupy her thoughts. "To sail from Jorvik to Dublin?"

"We will not take to the sea," he replied. "Not here. We will travel through Northumberland instead and cross the Irish Sea from a landing place near the Mersey."

And there were too many things writhing about within her, then. There were all her personal feelings about returning to Dublin. Her brother's face that she usually strove not to think about at all kept flashing in her head. Over and over again, twisted into one of his rages. But truly looking at all of that felt too huge. Too overwhelming.

So she focused on what Ulfric was saying instead. And what he was not saying. Well did she know, as did everyone, that ships sailed daily for Dublin from Jorvik. And so, too, did ships arrive from Dublin and far-off countries besides. From what she could recall of the conversations that had taken place in her hearing while they had ignored her and her muteness so resolutely back in the early days of her slavery, that had been the entire point. To create a channel between Sitric in Dublin and Ragnall in Northumberland.

There was no reason at all that Ulfric should cross the wilds of Northumberland to sail from its west coast instead.

Unless, that was, he did not wish for anyone to know what it was he did.

"You are doing your King's bidding," she said.

Ulfric did not exactly laugh at that, though the way he shifted how he stood made her think he might have. And not because he thought anything was amusing, she was certain.

"I must always do my King's bidding," he returned in a growl. "It is my duty and my honor. And a man without honor is no man at all."

"It is your duty and honor to return to Dublin, then?"

He moved closer and she could see the leashed violence in him. She would never know what was in her that thrilled to it when she had known violent men and liked them little. *You do know*, a voice in her challenged her. *It is that he controls himself, always. That he never acts in anger.*

Maybe that was so. But when he was like this, any sane woman would be afraid. Eithne was sure of it. Yet she was exhilarated.

He roamed closer still and then reached out, hooking a finger into the bodice of her dress and then deeper still, so he could tug at the top of the rope harness he'd made. Then haul her toward him.

"Thank me," he ordered her. "For deigning to return you from whence you came."

"Because that is every girl's dearest dream," she threw right back at him, not so much undaunted as... delighted. For Ulfric in this mood was like a storm. And even as a child, when Feargal and Fainche and the others had hidden away from the storms that pummeled Dublin, Eithne had liked to stand out in them. To feel the lash of the rain and wind on her face. Maybe this were no mystery after all. "To be carried off by a slaving Northman, the enemy of her people, and then returned, unharmed. Nothing but his thrall."

"My favor is no small thing," he said in a low voice, even as he reached down and pulled her dress up, tugging it over her head and then her shift too, so that she stood before him in nothing but the ropes he'd wound around her. "There are those who would scrap for my notice in the dirt and mud."

The way his eyes gleamed then made her legs feel weak. But she tipped her chin up, better to feel the howl of the storm upon her face. "They will call me a traitor. And they will be right."

"I tire of the petty outrage of the weak," Ulfric growled as he traced the ropes that even now dug into her skin, but just enough. He had experimented with ropes before, and she liked them. She liked them far too much. And liked better still when he untied her, yet the marks of the ropes remained. But he did not untie her now, and she found she liked this most of all.

He ran his hands over her breasts, and she knew he was fully aware that tying them as he had made them feel more engorged. Swollen, and near painful with sensation. She thought it pleased him. That the twist of his lips told her so.

He plucked at her nipples, his fingers deliberately rough. She knew better than to jerk away, for that would only encourage him. He was like hot metal in the fire. It was almost impossible not to reach out and press into it, the sensation so intense she wanted to live in it and hide from it at once. That was why he sometimes tied her down so he could do as he liked. But there were always tests, and this was one of them—could she stand still while he teased her nipples into hard, aching points?

Sometimes her reward was his mouth. Today, he seemed content to continue plying her with too much sensation. And like every other time he had returned from seeing Ragnall, she could not quite read his mood.

Was he calling her weak? Somehow she did not think he was, or not directly, but it was difficult to concentrate with those demanding fingers on her breasts, making her grit her teeth and curl her toes.

"When men dream of peace what they dream of, in truth, is gold," Ulfric told her, his voice harsh and his dark gaze alight. "And in these dreams, they do not stop to ask themselves how it is they came upon this gold to buy their glorious ships and sail across the seas to lands uncluttered by kings and claims. But I will tell you, little slave. Gold comes hard-won in battle, cities set alight and wars that never end. Gold requires blood. This is how it has always been. This is who we are."

"When women dream of peace," she replied softly, "they dream of nursing fat babies in a quiet place, where they hear the clash of no men's swords and need not fear that at any moment, the walls might be sacked, the village burned. That is who *we* are, Ulfric."

He raised his gaze from her breasts and it was so breathtakingly intense that it speared into her, as sure as any battle lance.

"You are not a traitor because you were taken, Eithne," he told her, his voice a dark pulse, like thunder. "This is your lot. I am your fate."

And something in her coiled tight at that, then made her shudder, down deep.

"You might as well throw stones at the moon as seek to escape me," he continued, the storm rolling through her as he spoke. "It will never work, for I will always find you. And know this now, Eithne. I will kill any man who tries to take you from me with my own hands. With nothing but pleasure."

"And if it is I who take me from you?" she asked, though she was breathless.

"You already know what punishments you risk." His hard mouth curved. "Do not think it will go any better for you a second time."

He tweaked her nipple then, hard enough to make her yelp. And yet even as he did, a rush of sensation seemed to arrow straight down from the pain of it to pool between her legs. Telling her exactly who she was.

Who she had always been, for this man alone.

Still she took a moment to study him. And to think about what he was telling her, in the murky way everyone within the King's reach seemed to speak. Using words without giving them their true meaning. That he needed to go to Dublin, yes. But did he fear she might have some allies there? Did he worry that if she ran from him again, it might be to those who would stand against him?

She almost laughed at that. She almost opened her mouth and disabused him of that notion, for she had no allies. Those who loved her were long dead. There was only her brother, and he was no ally. No small part of her hoped his bargain had not worked, and whatever silver he'd garnered from selling her had not saved his skin.

But before she could tell these things to Ulfric, she bit her tongue. Hard. And then had to ask herself what the matter was with her. What would make her think she should forget, for even a moment, who this man was to her?

Why would she hand him a weapon he could use against her—especially when she knew well he would do just that?

And again, that braided wanting wrapped tight

around her, feeling more and more like a knot at her throat by the second. Making the actual ropes she wore seem like a caress in comparison.

"Ulfric," she whispered anyway, surrendering herself to him yet again, "I don't think—"

But he slid a hand up to her throat, and the sheer glory of it stopped her words. For the rope hugged her tight, she was tangled in these braids of wanting, and now his hands were on her besides It was too much. She felt as if she were the gold he'd spoken of, molten hot at his touch, turned to liquid he could pour to make into molds as he chose.

In that moment, she wanted nothing more than to be the gold this man fought for across all these lands. Across any lands. For no matter how many battles he fought, he would come back to her, and there would be this. There would always be this.

At this moment, she wanted to pick out the pots from their own fire and press them into her skin, so she, too, could be scarred by the force of this thing between them. This unreasonable, unforgettable fire.

For the welts would fade. The bruises always healed. No matter how she loved each one, pressing her fingers into them beneath her clothes, because they were her secrets, and each hint of a sting was a gift. A reward.

Every time she sat, every time her movement made her skirts shift over her bottom, the discomfort reminded her of all the ways she was his.

And it was still not enough. It wasn't that she wanted

to look the part of a slave, as some did. Like the women with shorn hair she'd seen sometimes, from distant ports, so that any who looked upon them would know at once what they were. Maybe that was what she'd been struggling with all this time. She disliked being a slave, as anyone would.

But despite herself, and though it galled her, she still liked so very much being *his* slave.

"Tell me," he said, his hands around her throat so that her face was tipped up to his, "how many times will the staff kiss you this day?"

And she hated him and yet she loved him. She was filled with longing and with grief. She could not imagine returning to Dublin so many years into this slavery, and some part of her wanted to run. To take once more to the forests she'd known with Osthryth, because surely it was a shame too great to bear to see a place she had once known well while so firmly in the possession of this man. It was different here. It was different where there were only strangers, and his people. What did she care what they should think of her?

But in Dublin, there would be those who knew her. And worse, those who had known her parents, and would know how distraught they both would have been at such a dishonor. To her. To them. To their name.

At the same time, she wished there was some way she could but close her eyes only to open them and find herself already there. Finally on the same earth her brother walked. Finally close enough to him to repay him in kind for what he'd done to her.

It was too much. She felt everything, all of it. And there was something hectic and wild inside her that matched that glitter in his gaze, that air about him that suggested he felt the same things himself.

Because of course he did, she thought. For they were nothing if not inextricably bound up in each other, for good or ill. She knew that much was true, no matter which one of them was the master and which the slave. They were only these things to each other.

"Twenty," she said. She felt his grip tighten. Those dark eyes of his widened but slightly. "I want twenty marks upon me this night."

To remind her what she had been through. To mark well where they were headed. So she could think of little else in the coming days.

She thought he would argue.

Instead, Ulfric turned her around to face the bed. Then he took his time, winding more rope around her arms so they were bent behind her, making her grip her own elbows in such a way that her breasts jutted forward even more in the rope harness.

He stood back when he was done, admiring his own handiwork. He turned her this way, then that, so he could see it from all sides. Then he piled his furs high in the center of the bed and bent her over the side, propping her up against them, because he loved nothing more than putting her body at new angles.

But she loved it just as well. She was already trembling and slick between her legs.

"Let us return to where we began," he told her, and she had to fight to pay him close attention, for all she could hear was the pounding of her heart and the relentless slap of the staff against his palm. "You have asked for twenty blows this night. And you will take them all, but silently. Thank me for my consideration, then say no more."

"Thank you, Master," Eithne whispered.

And then she shut her eyes and tried her best not to brace herself against that first blow.

For she knew well that this was a gift. But she couldn't tell any longer if she was the one giving the gift of her surrender to him, or if he was the one gifting her with this beautiful, exquisite agony, for in the end, it was theirs.

The deeper the pain, the better the suffering.

The greater her surrender, the deeper their joy.

The circle never ended. Nor would it. Whether they were here or in Dublin, lost at sea, or even apart. For she understood that, too, here in these mad moments before the first blow landed. In the glory of her anticipation.

He had been right. She could have told Osthryth that she dared not set foot in Jorvik, and she should have. Anyone else would have. Only a fool would have imagined that she could walk into the city where he lived, stay here for days right under his nose, and somehow escape his notice.

In the clarity of these final seconds before the pain began—that beautiful pain she'd missed so much out in the woods that sometimes, when she was alone, she'd bruised her own flesh just to feel the faintest echo of it—she admitted the truth.

She would not have walked up to him and asked to be taken back into captivity. But she had hoped he would find her. Even though, the moment he had, she had fought and she had hated it. Because it all came down to that same simple truth.

She hated being a slave. But she loved being his.

And then, with only that short whistle in the air as a warning, the staff landed on her bottom, still red and sore from last night.

The pain bloomed white-hot.

And soon enough, Eithne thought no more.

It was one thing to struggle to thank him, to count. But he had freed her of that responsibility, and now all she had to do was feel.

Counting was its own quandary. It was more inter-active. It kept her from losing herself. For this was a bliss so sharp, so impossibly red and huge, it ate her up from the inside out.

He was a master at it, in truth, laying down one blow after the next with wicked precision. He did not hit a single welt from the night before, but rather laid a path around them. Then he worked his way along the backs of her thighs before he turned inward, that mad fire consuming her, changing her, teaching her more than she wished to know.

It was all pain. Only pain.

And she loved it.

Eithne moved her hips, but not to get away. To somehow get closer, get more. She felt like a bird, as if she had wings despite the fact she was bound—or perhaps because she was. Somehow that was connected in a way that seemed obvious without access to words. For she was tied up so securely in his ropes. And yet every stroke of that staff sent her further and further into a sky so blue, so clear, so perfect, she wanted to cry.

Perhaps she was, salt and water on her cheeks, and still he worked. Still he laid out one beautiful stripe after the next along the inner line of her thighs, moving closer and closer to her upturned heat, shiny with need.

And she knew. She had lost count, but she knew when he paused. She knew what was next.

Eithne flew higher and higher. She felt as if she was splayed out wide, wings spanning the heavens, instead of tied up, tipped over.

She flew and she waited, and that glorious, quivering bright red sensation was all she was now, all she wanted, all she could ever be—

And then Ulfric laid down that final kiss with scalding precision, right into the center of her woman's flesh.

And everything Eithne was…no more.

She was free.

Far away, she heard the echo of a scream, the rumble of her favorite voice.

But she flew away, unencumbered, unhindered by the stark earth, the caprice of fate, the trudge of one season into the next. She flew and she flew.

When she came back, she found herself propped up between his legs in her favorite position, her head against his thigh, his fingers in her hair. Here she was safe. Here she was protected. Here it did not matter where she'd gone or how she'd gotten there.

She could smell the herbs he used in his salve and moved just slightly, just enough to feel the sinuous ripple of all twenty marks he had laid upon her tonight. All of them sang out their own white-hot songs, and for a while, that was enough.

But eventually, she found the will to open her eyes. She made her way back into her body to find the ropes still holding her snug. She tested her arms and found them still held securely behind her, and then relaxed into the simple peace that brought her.

She was held tight. She was kept safe. No flight was too far.

"Welcome back," came his voice from above her.

Eithne was still too overwhelmed to speak, so she only rubbed her face against his thigh and heard that deep rumble within him. It was like the purr of an enormous cat, and so she did it again. And then again.

The more she rubbed herself into him, the more she felt. The pain, yes. But she liked that. There was also the salt on her lips that she knew meant she must truly have sobbed. The catch in her throat that told her she had screamed. But more, there was the aching hunger between her legs. Even though there was a part of her that quailed at the thought, remembering that last, bright shot, slashing directly into the center of her need.

But the more she thought of it, the more it made her squirm, until she shifted herself around so she could gaze up at him imploringly.

He looked down at her solemnly, his face grave. His big hands cradled her cheek as his thumb moved almost restlessly over her lips. He did not give her permission to speak.

And so, wordlessly, she beseeched him.

For he had not allowed her to pleasure him this way since she'd returned. He had told her from the first that she must earn it, and he'd meant it. He would take her in any number of inventive ways, but never allow her this.

She had heard women speak disparaging of the things men liked to do with their little swords. The places they liked to put them and the ways they expected a woman to anoint them.

And she had never understood.

Because it had always been as much her pleasure as his.

Quietly, she begged him.

And on the next pass of his thumb over her lips, he dipped it into the seam there and then pressed it against her tongue.

She sucked him in, greedy and grateful at once. He moved his thumb in and out of her lips, a pale substitute for what she wanted, yet still its own gift. She sucked on it as she could, determined not to waste it.

Soon enough he set her away from him, and she hissed a little as her bottom hit her bare feet as she sat back on her heels. All the welts on the backs of her thighs and legs folded into each other and bloomed.

But the pain made her feel edgy. Alive.

And so hungry she didn't know what to do with herself.

He stared down at her, forbiddingly.

Then slowly, Ulfric reached between his legs and pulled himself free. And Eithne shook. The shaking began from somewhere deep inside of her, connected to all the pain and the way it bloomed straight into that greedy ache between her legs. She shook, and she knelt up. She searched his gaze, waiting. And waiting still.

And then, finally, let the relief sweep over her when he nodded, very slowly.

Ulfric settled back down in his chair. And she was so greedy, but she tried to go slow as she lowered herself forward, her body straining. As she leaned in and licked the very tip of him, reveling in the salt she found there, the rough musk, all man.

All *him*.

This was a dance she'd done so many times, and yet it felt new. She felt emotion welling in her eyes again, that she should be back here. That she should be bound this time, so beautifully. Rope everywhere, so that as she licked her way down the length of him, then found her way up once more to take him deep into her mouth, she felt as if he was the one who held her. Who led her.

And sure enough, he only allowed her one deep slide on her own before his hands found her head. He took his time wrapping his fist into her hair, and then he was guiding her in truth. Pulling her off-balance, so that her knees were on the ground but everything else was at his will. At his bidding.

And this was a different kind of wings than before. A different sort of flight.

Rather than off into that wild sky inside herself, this journey was all about Ulfric.

The scent of him in her nose, his taste in her mouth and down the back of her throat. The way he thrust into her, never letting her find his pace or match his strokes. Keeping her off-balance while holding her perfectly still.

And Eithne supposed that this was the closest a woman ever got to the glory men sung about. To give herself over in this way, to do her duty like this, to make herself an instrument for her master's use, did not make her feel like a martyr. It did not feel wicked at all.

When she was away from him, she would remember scenes like this and assure herself he was a devil.

But here, now, she knew better.

This was sacred.

And it was theirs.

And when he finally groaned and held her fast, pulsing deep into her throat, she drank him down and felt complete.

He held her like that for some time, and then another groan came from him, seemingly torn from his great wide chest. He lifted her up, upending her once more, but this time he was tossing her onto the bed.

Then they were in his furs together and he was tugging at the ropes, setting her free so that the blood rushed back in and made her ache. So intense it made her head spin and then seem to sink straight to that soft heat between her thighs.

She wrapped her arms around him and locked her ankles in the small of his back as he pumped himself into her, so huge it would have hurt if she was not so molten hot already. And it was almost too much, the way he crowded her and plunged so deep, taking her over. The way the weight of him bore her down, setting every mark he'd put upon her on fire.

It was almost too much.

And that was when he lowered his face to hers, and then, finally kissed her.

With his hard, cruel, beautiful mouth.

Deep and wild. Like he might never stop.

Like he was making a solemn vow.

Again and again, until they both catapulted off into the dark. Together.

Much later, he woke her up and she found that while

she'd slept, he'd packed up their belongings and had produced bowls of stew, no doubt from the King's hall.

"Eat," he told her gruffly. "You will need your strength come morning."

After they cleaned their bowls, they bathed together before the fire and Ulfric combed out her hair with his fingers. Then braided it to his preference.

And then ruined his work by taking her into his bed once more, kissing her until they were both half-mad and panting. Then he rolled her above him so she might ride them both into all that joy.

Eithne could not count the number of times he woke her that night. It was lost in the delirium of his tongue in her mouth and his cock deep inside her body, so that she was utterly possessed and utterly his, just as she wanted it. And in case she forgot, there were always her welts to hold on to, so he could make her gasp a little, or a lot, then shatter all the harder.

Again and again he came to her, and turned them both inside out.

And in the morning, they rose before dawn, climbed onto his horse, and started their long trek home.

Chapter Eleven

Ulfric had bid his farewells to his King before they left. When Ragnall had entrusted his message to Ulfric and he, in turn, had accepted his King's trust as the gift it was.

Ulfric would guard it with his life.

It was Leif who rode out with them in the morning and stayed with them until the sun reached its midday height.

"I will see you again, cousin," Ulfric had said gruffly when the time came for his cousin to go his own way.

"If the gods allow," Leif replied with his usual laugh. "And even if they do not in this life, it is a certainty we will drink together in the next."

They pounded each other on the back and then Leif had headed away. Not back toward Jorvik, but farther north on another of their King's errands.

"Will he become Ragnall's favorite?" Eithne asked. "Now that you and your brother are no longer at his side?"

"He is already one of the King's favorites," Ulfric replied, gruffly.

But then he relented, because she sat before him on his horse. And that was a temptation in itself, delicious beyond measure. He could feel the way she shifted, no doubt trying to find some comfortable way to sit on a horse between his thighs, with all the welts she had sustained and the way he'd reddened her bottom anyway.

Just imagining the beauty of those marks pleased him well. It made his cock press against her, which in turn made her squirm all the more. He cast an eye over the trees at the side of the road, thinking how easy it would be to take her behind them and gorge himself on her anew...

And yet he intended to ride hard this day. He told himself that waiting would make it all the sweeter when they stopped and he could enjoy her fully.

"My cousin heads north," he told Eithne as he rode on. "For where there are enemies of Wessex, there, too, is the possibility of new friends."

And that was one benefit of Edward of Wessex's endless march to claim the whole of this island. He made more enemies by the day.

Eithne made a low noise. "How far north?"

He could hear in her question the usual fear of the Scots.

"Of all of us, Leif is the most diplomatic." Ulfric found himself smiling, and was as glad she could not see it. "Too many mistake his laughter and think him unthreatening. If anyone can weave a peace with the vicious Scots, it is Leif."

Eithne twisted around to look back at him, her eyes wide. "And if he cannot?"

Ulfric kicked the horse beneath them so she had no choice but to turn toward the front again, then hold on, her question left unanswered.

But he thought of little else that day. He and his brother and cousin had been together always. Even now Thorbrand might well be lost at sea, as so many were, on the passage across the brooding sea to distant Ísland. Though Ulfric knew his brother to have both a way with ships and the gods' favor, that was no guarantee. There were no guarantees, ever. Leif headed to certain death up north. Thorbrand headed for uncertainty abroad. Ulfric, too, could do nothing but Ragnall's bidding, for these were the oaths he'd taken. This was how he lived. And neither his brother nor his cousin would thank him should he attempt to sway them from their duties, nor shame them by neglecting his own.

But no one had ever said that the right thing to do, the honorable thing to do, would also be the easy thing.

He rode hard. And when he stopped, late into the long evening, he set up their camp quickly in a protected clearing in the forest. He fed them both dried meat from the pouches he carried, and then took advantage of their isolation and the forest to indulge himself in her, long after darkness fell.

The next morning, he was near enough to cheerful that

he hardly recognized himself. But then, this was how he recalled Eithne. These were his fondest recollections—long days of travel, longer nights in his tent. Such had been their earliest time together. So too were these days bright and long, summer fair and sweet. And the nights yet a greater gleam.

On the third day of their ride, the weather began to change and by that afternoon, the rain began to fall.

Ulfric had been avoiding the villages and he suspected she knew why, though she declined to ask. The fewer who saw them, the better. For there could only be secrets between dead men, or none, as Ragnall liked to say.

He tried to push on through the storm as he would have done alone. And Eithne did not complain. Perhaps that was why he stopped early, throwing up his tent under the cover of the thick trees in the forest.

She crawled inside while he made his horse comfortable, then he crawled in after her. Then paused, because she was lying on her back, her hands thrown over her head, smiling as the rain pounded against the roof of his tent. She looked over at him and smiled wider. As if she had forgot who they were.

He liked it far more than he should.

Almost as if he wanted—

But he thrust that thought aside.

"I love the rain," she said. "Particularly in the forest."

He started to ask her what she knew of forests and rain, but stopped himself. Once again, he'd forgotten.

All those many months he had been without her. He wore her mark on his face and yet still he forgot, when it had near to ruined him before he'd discovered her in Jorvik.

Yet he could not seem to work up his usual temper about these matters today. With that smile on her face and her arms thrust over her head, like an invitation to joys he could not quite name. He wanted to reach for her.

He could not have said why he did not.

Eithne's gaze moved over his face. She turned over on her side, propping herself up so she could look at him.

"Osthryth and I would forage in forests just like this one. And we had no tent, so I became used to being fair sodden whenever the weather turned. It's only the getting wet that irritates. Once you are already soaked through, what does it matter if you become more so?"

"I would not have thought foraging would be to your taste."

She wrinkled up her nose as she looked at him. "There cannot always be meat in the pot, as my mother used to tell us. Yet God still provides. If you are a good forager, there will always be a decent meal to fill the belly."

Ulfric reached over and traced the rope beneath her dress. He tied her into it every morning now, taking his time over the placement of the knots. Some days tightening in one place, some days another. They did not discuss it. He was not sure why he thought they ought to. It was no more than another ritual, and well did they both honor it. He liked knowing that he held her at all times. She liked feeling it. He knew this in the flush of pleasure that overtook her each morning as she ran her hands over the harness, as if memorizing the placement of the ropes, before she pulled on her shift. And again when he took the ropes off her each evening did she reach for the red marks the ropes left on her fair skin, smiling slightly.

In this way, that spark between them danced ever higher, all the time.

Still, it was an odd thing to realize that he thought of her only as the slave he had so carefully trained since the day he'd bought her, when he knew well that there was more to her. For this dance of theirs revealed character above all else. He knew she had fortitude. He knew she had a deep, abiding fire in her, not only the one they shared between them. She was not afraid of him, for one, which distinguished her from most. More, she was not afraid to provoke him to get what she wanted— and while he laughed at that and punished her for it in as delectable a fashion as he could, he recognized her for who she was.

Formidable in her own way. A warrior by rights, though perhaps only he knew it.

Maybe she is wasted as no more than a concubine, something in him whispered.

"I find myself surprised by you," he told her, though

the words felt forced from within him. Surely he should have known better than to speak them aloud. "I cannot say I like it."

"It is not your fault." Her voice was soft and yet serious, as if she, too, had forgotten her place. "I am surprised by you, also. It is because, though we spent years together, we did not speak. So the things we feel we know of each other may be true enough, but there are many details missing that only words can fill."

He tugged a little on the rope, pinching it between his fingers through her dress and smiling faintly when he heard her breath change. "My ears must deceive me. I thought I was nothing to you but the cruel Northman who bought you in a Dublin market."

She laughed, and he did not mistake that for anything less the momentous thing it was.

Because she was in fact his slave, and he knew well that it could not matter how close he felt to her. Given the opportunity, and enough rope, she would always tie him to the bed and cut him on her way out.

He even understood it now.

Ulfric couldn't say when that had happened. Now, as the rain fell down all around them, he fingered that scar on his cheek and knew only that the deep temper that had lived in him all the time she was gone had subsided. Not as if it had disappeared entirely, or ever would, but it had changed. It had shifted.

He was not sure he wanted to dig into that any deeper.

"You are cruel," she agreed, but with that gleam of heat in her gaze. "There can be no denying that." Almost idly, he pinched one of her nipples and she made a satisfying squeaking sound. "But I already knew that. Lately I have come to know other things. I knew that Thorbrand was your brother and Leif your cousin, and that all of you were kin in some way. But is only of late that I truly understood that you were essentially all raised together by Ragnall."

"We will ever be on opposite sides, little slave." He pinched her nipple again to watch the bloom of red flowers in her cheeks. "The Northman scourge your kings tossed out of Ireland are my family and friends."

"And the Irish your family and friends killed on your return were mine," she replied softly.

"But this is the way of it," he told her, yet not as if he was handing down a judgment, as he would have done before. It was different today. Perhaps it was the rain, the drum of it, working its way beneath his skin. It made him wish for her to understand above all else. "This is the world we live in. We claim what we can and make the best of what we have. There is an honor in that, I think. If you do your duty. If you keep your vows."

"Free men make vows," she said softly. "A slave girl has ropes in place of them, but I take your meaning all the same."

He felt the change between them, too sudden for his liking. For she had laughed only moments before, but now the spark had flared and then turned, and he could feel the cut of it.

For it occurred to him that in all the ways he knew her, in ways most men could not dream of knowing a woman, there was one thing he could never know. He could make assumptions. He had. He could discern what her body wanted, what it craved and desired, feared and longed for at once, and so he did. He still believed that she would never have set foot in Jorvik, knowing he was there, if there was not some part of her that did not wish for him to find her.

Yet of all the things he could know about her, he could never know one simple truth: whether or not she would ever come to him of her own free will.

That moved through him like a thunderclap, though the rain that fell outside gave no hint of that kind of storm. The rain poured down, but it were not Thor riding into battle, his chariot pulled by Tanngrisnir and Tanngnjóstr and his hammer, mighty Mjölnir, flashing bright light across the heavens and defeating his foes with every throw.

That was only happening within him, perhaps a message from the gods he did not wish to receive.

Eithne's gaze went quizzical, and he knew every shade of green there. Yet he still could not know the answer to that one question.

When he knew, then, that truly, it was the only question that mattered.

He lifted his hand and set it to the side of her face.

And something crested in him, some kind of frantic wave like the North Sea in winter, filled with rage and fury yet more beautiful for it.

He had no idea what he meant to say, only that it needed saying, that it burned in him like a new hunger. A need within him, sharp like breath.

Yet even as he opened his mouth to say it, he froze.

"Ulfric?" Eithne asked, her voice hushed.

But he was already moving, for he had heard a sound that did not fit with the rain-soaked forest on the other side of the tent's walls, with or without the intrusion of the gods. He was already moving and his sword was in his hand as if it drew itself. He pushed his way through the tent's opening and out into the wet and damp.

He saw nothing, but he knew what he had heard. And he melted into the trees, keeping his ears pricked, his footfalls so light it was as if he made no sound at all.

As if he was a part of the rain, as one with the trees.

He waited.

Behind the trunk of a tree, he quieted his breath. And with it the pounding of his heart, already anticipating the coming fight.

He waited.

And then he heard it again. The faint, yet unmistakable sound of a foot touching down in the undergrowth.

Ulfric moved again, everything in him going still and unforgiving. He picked his way toward the sound, tracking his quarry with deadly intent.

And then, at last, he saw the figure in the damp,

moving from behind a tree with a stick in its hands and all its attention focused forward.

On the tent where he had only recently been lying down, heedless, as if asking for an ambush.

He melted his way closer, as if he were no more than another bit of rain, yet as he did, he saw movement at the entrance to the tent. His jaw turned to steel. Surely he had ordered Eithne to stay put, but even if he hadn't, did that not go without saying? That she should remain safe when any and all enemies lurked nearby? He wanted to call out and order her to remain in the tent but if he did, he would alert the ragged, filthy creature he saw before him to his location.

In the clearing, Eithne pushed free of the tent and stood. He watched her with no small part of his attention—and dismay—as she looked around, taking in their would-be attacker and Ulfric not ten paces behind.

Her eyes widened in alarm. Ulfric lifted his sword high, prepared to handle this threat decisively—

But Eithne screamed.

"Ulfric!" she cried out, already throwing herself across the clearing. *"No!"*

And though he could not credit it as a possibility, this woman he continued not to know at all lunged into the forest. Did she think to rescue *him*?

But no, she was about a greater madness—throwing herself between the creature he had every intention of cutting down and his sword.

It took him a long moment to understand she meant to ward him off.

"Eithne," he bit out. "Step aside."

"This is my friend!" Her hands were outstretched, palms toward him as if she could hold him back herself, with all her puny strength. "You cannot kill her!"

Ulfric scowled at the creature she protected, that he had thought no more than a desperate troll, whether a person or not. But then the rags and dirt seemed to rearrange themselves, and he realized that this was the old woman from the market square. The true crone.

No troll in truth, but a woman who dared to glare at him with an equal amount of the disgust he felt sure were all over his face.

"Step aside," she cried, her eyes bright with hatred aimed straight at Ulfric. "I'm going to kill him."

"With what?" Ulfric demanded. "Dirt and fleas?"

The old woman sneered at him. "I hear you take a dagger well, Northman." And as he watched as she produced, from the depths of her ragged garments, a crude dagger of her own.

Ulfric but laughed. He stood straight and sheathed his sword. Then he lifted both hands out before him as if in surrender. "I bid you try, hag."

"Ulfric!" came Eithne's voice, but now she struggled as much to keep the old woman from lunging at him as to keep him from swinging his blade.

"Some call me a witch," the old woman said, with a cackle. "I need only nick you with this dirty flea of mine. No need to posture and pretend and wave a great blade as if it might make up for the tiny dagger betwixt your legs. The poison will do the rest."

He only shook his head. "You think highly of yourself indeed, witch or no, if you think you might do a single thing to me without my wishing it."

The woman only laughed again, in a manner Ulfric knew she meant to unnerve him. He would not describe himself thus, so much as watchful. Careful. For one thing he knew well was that women, while never the warriors men were, because of the limits of their size and their strength, could nonetheless be surprisingly deadly. For they were ever unpredictable. Almost as if they did not expect to win and thus, perhaps because of that, had nothing to lose. And so would do things a man would not.

"Stop taunting each other," Eithne bit out, but she seemed now flushed with temper more than fear. She turned her glare on the old woman and was yet still glaring when she turned back to him.

Ulfric did but lift his brow, and she flushed. As he watched, she fought to adjust her expression, but he would still describe the look on her face as a frown. At him, which could not bode well for her.

"I will kill him," the older woman was saying, as if Ulfric, four times her size and more powerful than ten of her, was not right there before her. "You escaped him once, child. You can do it again. And this time, you and I will make certain he will not rise to claim you once more."

Ulfric dropped his hands. He crossed his arms, then watched his slave's face. Too closely, perhaps.

For he had never considered himself a sentimental man. Not even when he was deep in his cups, though some men drank themselves to misery. But he found his chest felt tight as he saw the indecision in Eithne's gaze.

And there it was, yet again.

He wanted her to want him. He wanted her to choose him, even here, when there was no real choice to be made. This old woman was no threat to him, no matter if she had anointed her puny knife with every witch's poison in the land. He could disarm her, snap her neck, and end the situation without even breaking a sweat.

And would have, would it not upset Eithne.

Eithne. His slave. And yet there was that tightness around him, as if he wore his own ropes yet made of steel, and he thought he would die before he let Eithne know such a truth. He had half a mind to gut himself, here and now, for the treacherous thought alone.

"Ulfric," she said, and much as he liked his name in her mouth, there was another name he liked better. He found his temper far thinner that ought to have been in the face of this game. "Osthryth is my friend. Were it not for her aid, I would have died. She found me wandering the woods, cold and wet, and she nursed me back to health."

"Did she indeed." He swept a gaze over the old

woman, who bared her teeth at him in return, then looked back to Eithne. "And why was it you were in those woods in the first place, I wonder?"

She had the sense, or the shame, to flush a deeper red. "It hardly matters how I came to be there."

"Does it not? Are you sure? For I will tell you that few things matter more to me."

The old woman spat. "Well did I teach her a thing or two, once I saved her from certain death. This time, she will gut you like a fish."

Osthryth made as if to hurl herself at him, but Eithne moved with her and struggled to keep her from it.

"Please," Eithne said, urgently. "*Please*, Ulfric. I cannot leave her behind."

His head tipped to one side. "And what is it you ask of me, little slave?" He ignored the growling sound the old woman made at the name he called her. "You want me to let this creature travel with us? Will I sleep with one eye open, waiting for her poisoned blade to sink between my ribs? Will I suffer her insults day and night? No man would stand against me were I to strike her down where she stands. For she is here for one purpose only. To steal what is mine."

The old woman launched into further invective, but Ulfric saw only Eithne. He saw the misery in her green gaze, and how she implored him. And how, too, she clearly knew what a risk it was to even ask him things. To stand against him in any way.

She was a slave. She had no right to anything he did

not give her of his own hands. There were some who would have been outraged that she dared ask at all. Some would already have killed the old woman for her temerity and beat the slave who dared ask that he consider her feelings at all.

A beating that would not end in her moans of pleasure, her body open and willing.

Ulfric knew there were no rational reason he should even consider such a request. For there was no benefit to him. There was no reason he should suffer another moment of the hag's noxious company.

Yet he could not help but think that if he let this happen, it might…gain him the favor of the slave girl whose *favor* was surely irrelevant. He had already bought it. He already owned her.

Still, there was that hunger in him. He wanted more. Not just her surrender on his terms, for he had that. He had always had that.

He wanted her surrender on her terms, too.

He told himself it was simply more of the same thing, and this would only make it deeper. Better. For him, which ought to have been his only concern.

It was possible that Eithne had bewitched him after all.

Before him, he could see her tremble faintly, for she must know that she would pay for this—and how. In her eyes, that impossible green, he read the kind of begging he liked best and a hint of resolve, too. As if, were he to demand it now, she would fling herself at his feet.

Ulfric knew it was her pride that kept her from it, and a new truth dawned in him. For he discovered that he liked well how proud she was. He had glimpsed it that day in the slave market and it had never left her. He loved nothing more than watching her swallow her pride—for him. Only and ever for him.

He did not wish to see her humble herself before anyone else. Ragnall was one thing. This old woman was another, and he did not need her to tell him that it was this that would hurt her more.

There was only one sort of hurt he liked to inflict upon her. This was not it.

Slowly, Ulfric inclined his head, giving her his assent.

He watched her breath come then, big gulps of air as if she had gone without.

"It will cost you," he told her, his voice hard. Only then did he shift his gaze to the old woman. "And if this creature does not find herself some manners, the cost will be dear indeed."

Chapter Twelve

Eithne could not fathom how it was that Osthryth yet lived. That Ulfric had not yet struck her down where she stood, bristling with umbrage, as if she were in truth the witch she pretended she was.

"I am well," she whispered fiercely to her friend when Ulfric released her from the particular bond of his gaze. "I am not hurt." She was still holding Osthryth back from any sudden starts in Ulfric's direction, so she felt the tension in the old woman's body…shift.

"He is a Northman, as you said," Osthryth said, in a voice not low enough for Eithne's liking. For she knew too well that he was keeping count of all the insults laid before him this day. She would answer for them all, that was certain. She repressed a small shiver at the thought, and it was not of fear. "Yet he is not just any Northman. Men sing of Ulfric the Grim across the land, and it is not his kindness that inspires them. He took you for his slave, child."

"So he did." Eithne wished she knew what part of

her this was that wanted only to defend him, protect him, that she might cut it out. She saw his lips curve slightly at that and shivered all the more. But she aimed a frown at her friend as he stepped around them, the way he showed Osthryth his back, with such unconcern, an insult in itself. "Yet I tell you true, he is neither vicious nor cruel in the way you expect."

"But surely it was his cruelty you spoke of most, before," the old woman replied, a thoughtful look in her gaze.

Eithne looked away and hoped the heat she could feel in her cheeks was not as bright as it seemed.

Ulfric stalked back for the tent, while above, the rain eased. "If she will travel with us, she will not be armed," he said from across the clearing, in a tone Eithne knew all too well.

Her breath felt like its own shiver, inside and out.

"You have followed us all this way," she said to Osthryth. "And well do I love you for it. But you do not need to follow us further. If you do not wish to hand over your knives, I will not blame you and he will not stop you. You can go back to Jorvik, to your kin."

"Back to the sort of hospitality a dog would find a grievous insult?" Osthryth snorted. "I think not, child."

Eithne felt her hands curl into fists at her sides. "If you stay, you cannot cross him."

Osthryth looked close enough to amused. "Can I not?"

"This is my life," Eithne blurted out. Too intensely,

but then, she knew not how else to address this situation that should never have occurred. It had never crossed her mind that the two of them might meet. She felt…torn asunder. "A life he holds in the palm of his hand. There is no possibility that you could ever best him. And if you love me, Osthryth, you will spare me having to witness your death at his hand—those very same hands."

The old woman's gaze was too wise, and furious besides, but all she did was nod.

That night, Osthryth brought her old but reliable nag into the clearing. Then she made a show of throwing her various weapons at Ulfric's feet. Several daggers. A selection of sharpened sticks that could be used as spears or even lances, in a pinch. An axe. A pouch of foul-smelling herbs that Eithne knew were not poisonous, but Ulfric was meant to question. Instead, he gazed at Eithne with no little forbearance, the look in his eyes promising a particular retribution.

She swallowed hard and hid the shiver that ran down her back.

He built a fire now that the rain had passed and they sat around it in uneasy silence, Ulfric providing cheese and meat to Eithne while Osthryth ate seeds and nuts from her own stores.

But it was when they crawled into the tent again that set Eithne to trembling, and again, not in any fear.

The interior of the tent was surprisingly spacious. They had lived in it for two years while they had marched across Northumbria and there was room enough for all manner of activities, as well she knew. She had already become intimately acquainted with the wooden posts he had used to erect it.

But tonight, she knew Osthryth was nearby. That she slept as she always did, under her horse and a few skins treated in beeswax to keep the weather off. No tents for a woman at home in these woods, for she thought they encouraged softness. And there was no room for softness in a woman on her own, no matter how many thought her a witch.

Men only fear a witch to a certain point, Osthryth had told her once. *Then they claim she is an offense to their preferred magics and stone her dead.*

No witches would save Eithne tonight. When the tent's flaps were pulled tight and closed behind her, she sought out Ulfric's gaze in the gloom and she didn't think twice. She went straight to her knees.

If Osthryth saw the way she shook, the older woman would think it terror. But Eithne knew too well it was not. It was that deeper, richer anticipation. It was a shiver that wound around and around within her, lighting her up with that taut, terrible fire.

She could feel it everywhere, the lick of those flames. Her breasts already felt heavy and as they swelled with hunger, they pressed into the ropes that held her. That only intensified the sensation. It made everything inside her seem to rush straight down to that slick ache between her legs.

Where she burned even brighter.

Ulfric was silent, which only made it worse.

Or better, something in her acknowledged.

She had arranged their pallet earlier. Ulfric lounged there now, looking for all the world as if he were nothing but indolent. As if he were any warrior back from a battle won, lazing about in a merry hall as women vied to fill his cup.

Eithne sometimes wondered if that was how others saw him. For a certainty, he was sterner than some. Harsher than most. But surely they could not tell that he carried that ribbon of fire within him. Surely they did not know the wickedness that she now felt when he looked at her, as if it were a scent in the air. As unmistakable as smoke.

"Osthryth cares for me very much," she told him softly. Not quite begging. "Despite the promises she has made this night, I cannot be sure what she would do if she heard sounds to suggest that you were beating me. Or even turning to me as men do."

Ulfric only watched her narrowly. And the longer he kept his counsel, the more the clamor inside of her seemed to grow. Until her breath was coming as quickly as if she was already tossed over his lap, slowly growing warm and pliable beneath his uncompromising hand.

She felt too hot already.

"Do you imagine I fail to possess the ability to keep my pleasures to myself?" He shook his head in that way he did sometimes, as if he found this all amusing, this wildfire between them. The lightning strikes of his will and her surrender that sometimes seemed so bright and so dangerous she did not understand how it had not yet eaten her whole. "I find myself very nearly wounded that you think so little of me."

"No, no, Ulfric, I—"

"Tonight," he interrupted her, his voice low and smooth and more deadly than any dagger, "if I were you, that is not the name I would use."

Another lightning strike, making everything in her quiver. "That is not what I meant, Master," she whispered.

He studied her a moment, then lifted a hand to beckon she come closer. She stayed low to the ground and crawled to him, finding her way onto his furs and then between his outstretched legs. He was propped up, very nearly sitting, and she did not know why she should find this a greater wickedness than all that had come before.

Then again, perhaps she did know. It was that Osthryth was now here as witness. That the old woman could, for all she knew, have crept to the side of the tent to listen to what went on between Eithne and her captor. That she might listen to Eithne, who had once danced beneath the stars, her hair unbound and bare, call this man her master.

That same bright red shame that had eaten at her all the time she was apart from Ulfric.

Eithne felt it, as implacable as the tide coming in, but it wasn't all she felt.

For something in her settled, the way it always did, when she sat between his legs. When he reached over with one big hand to toy with her hair, the line of her jaw, her chin. More than that, there was the dance of flames within her, as relentless as its own tide, as if everything inside her was already turning into the thick honey she could feel pooling between her thighs.

"Look at you," Ulfric said, almost as if he marveled at what he saw before him. "It isn't that you do not want my hand upon you. It is that you do not want your friend to hear it land."

A different sort of light took over his gaze then. And Eithne felt herself as caught as if his hands had already closed over her neck. As if he could feel the way her throat ached because he hadn't done so already.

"I will have you say it," he said, his voice a low rumble.

"Please," she whispered, before she could think better of it. "Do not make me."

He sat up further, and he was so *big*. Sometimes the sheer might of him made her breathless. They were the both of them fully clothed now, and the way he touched her could even be called tender. If Osthryth had her face to any crack that let her peep within, she would see them look like nothing so much as simple, run-of-the-mill lovers.

That was its own shame, of course. And yet that was

not the reason that within her, Eithne's own dark heart beat too hard.

For there was a truth she had not thought she would have to face directly. Or she had hoped she would not. A truth that was the ache in her bottom as she knelt. It was the way she squirmed, just a little, so she could be sure to feel the marks he'd laid with such precision down the length of her thighs, covering them with welts that hurt, but variously. All day, she sat sometimes before him and sometimes behind him on his horse and felt them all.

Another truth was that it did not make her feel roughly used. It made her feel beautiful. Precious. That he should have so noted her absence that he found it necessary to transfer the marks he'd made to pass the days onto her flesh.

But more than that, she liked the pain.

And she knew that must make her a devil all her own, twisted and wicked, unfit to raise her head in the sight of God or decent people anywhere. Or even her old friend, who would never understand.

How could anyone understand? She hardly understood herself.

And Ulfric yet waited, his gaze given her no quarter. Allowing her nowhere to hide, nowhere to go.

And the fight within her only made her want him more. As if what she loved most was the struggle. This internal struggle to bend herself to his will because she knew where it led. Even though there was no easy way to get there.

She loved where it led, but she loved the pain, too. And that was the hardest to reckon with. For his blows might make her sob. The kiss of that staff could make her scream. He knew a thousand ways to make her hate him in the moment, to make her world disappear into that white-hot slash of heat and pain, but she loved that part, too.

She loved how huge it was within her, that pain. How it took her over, took her out of herself.

How it would give her wings, and set her free, and let her fly away into the very stars other people could only dance beneath.

He made her soar, and as her heart thumped hard within her chest—the force of all these realizations— Eithne recognized that beneath all of that was a deeper truth still.

He owned her. She was his property. His slave, and though her brother had tricked her and betrayed her, Ulfric had bought her fairly.

She should hate him or at least, feel nothing for him, because he was forever her slave master, whose wants and needs she was bound by law to place always above her own.

Even if he had been nothing but benevolent, she ought to detest him.

Eithne told herself she did. In those months she had escaped him, she had told herself little else. It was no wonder at all that Osthryth questioned her now, for she had spoken only of his many cruelties—though she had not listed them.

Because if she had, she would have had to explain too much.

She would have had to give herself away.

It wasn't just that she had this dark, wicked need for him within her. It wasn't just that he had somehow known, right from the start, how she would respond to him. He had bought her but more than that, he'd recognized her.

He had known all of this was within her and he had brought it to the surface with painstaking care.

She didn't hate him. Not even close.

The wickedest truth of all, the darkest secret she possessed, was that Eithne loved him.

The truth of that bloomed within her like the kiss of his staff at full power. It was worse than any pain. Brighter, hotter.

It lit her up.

She felt her body respond to it as if it were a physical blow.

And meanwhile, Ulfric only watched her, his dark eyes taking in all of it. The way her eyes glazed over. The way her lips parted. The heat she could feel move over her—and it took every bit of willpower she had not to jerk her chin out of his fingers, even though it made her toes curl to think what it was he could see on her face.

Still, he only waited.

Because he knew. Maybe not that this was the terrible truth she had just stumbled over, but the rest of it he knew as he had always known. It was this struggle that defined them both. And he knew nothing better than he knew a battlefield, whether it was some frigid, contested land in Northumberland, or her body itself.

"I… I…" Her throat was so dry. Her mouth did not feel like hers. But she could not bring herself to lie. "You're right. I don't want her to hear."

She watched that wicked smile kick up the corner of his hard mouth. "But you took far too long to answer, little slave. I am not satisfied."

He angled himself closer to her and then his fingers moved over her head, tugging at the braids he liked to put there himself. Little tugs, little flashes of sharpness that only primed her. It only made her think too much of the far greater pain he could inflict. And would.

"I do not think you are ever satisfied," she whispered.

And as she watched, that smile of his took over his face and stopped her heart for a moment.

For a man should not be beautiful, and yet that was the only word that fit.

"No, indeed, I am not," he agreed. "Nor will I ever be, I think."

He smoothed his fingers down her throat then, and both of them sighed a little as his hand found its place on her neck. Wrapping her up tight, holding her just right.

And it was all connected. It was all part of the same

tight grip. From the stripes of flame all up and down her thighs, to the pulsing ache at her core, to the ropes that held her tight and fast—digging into her flesh just enough that she could not take a single breath without feeling the bite of them—to the warmth and heat and mastery of his hand at her throat...

It all led to the same place.

She was his.

It was that simple, that profound.

Eithne could still remember, too clearly, when he had done that the first time. She had tried her best to go somewhere else inside herself. When he'd marched her away from the market that day, taking her to a small house that had once belonged to people she knew. Before Dublin had fallen. Back when the only real pain she had known was the loss of her family to an illness that had taken many others that vile winter.

She had fought to block out the part of her that witnessed what was happening as he stripped her down, rendering her naked before him, when no man had ever gazed upon her like that. Or worse, when he put her in that tub of his and then bathed her, so gently, confusing her greatly. For she had trembled at the sin of being so exposed and trembled further that he touched her as he had, putting his hands and that length of soft wool in places no one had ever touched. Places she had never touched herself.

Eithne had thought she ought to die from that alone, but even then she'd felt a sinful pleasure in it. She'd told herself at the time that it was relief, that was all, that her captor did not simply throw her skirts over her head and rut against her. She had known too well that any other one of those stinking, rough-edged men who had shouted and jeered and touched her would already have done so.

Everyone knew how men treated their female slaves. And yet she remembered how Ulfric had lain with her that first day, her body scrubbed clean, already feeling more like his than hers. He had lain with her and held her, that hand around her throat just like this, and somehow, she had not found a way to escape it, off inside herself. She had not managed to figure out how she could disappear.

They can take you, and likely will, one of the other women had told her as so many of them had huddled together, hoping to protect the children. And waiting, as women always waited, for the careless men shouting outside to have their battles. Waiting to see what would become of them when the fighting was done. *And if you cannot escape them, you escape as you must.*

She had tapped the side of her head, looking around the group of them, tucked away behind walls of mud and dung that would not keep the invaders at bay for long. Not if their own men fell. Not if the city was taken.

Some of the women were openly sobbing already. Some buried their heads, or held their children close, no doubt offering up their prayers. But Eithne had been rapt.

You let them do what they will, the other woman said. *For it is a certainty they will anyway and the more you fight, the more they will fight back. That is what they do. Better by far to keep their fighting to the battlefields. Lie still. Think of other things. And soon enough, it will be over.*

One of the much older women had cackled at that in that way the women did, though Eithne had not understood it back then. For she had still been so innocent. She had still known herself so little. She had known only that there was a wealth of knowledge about men's ways that all women knew, and must learn, but maids could but wonder what the sounds they heard at night from their parents' bed meant.

If they have been in the drink, it will be sooner even than that, the older woman had said, and the others had laughed along.

Eithne had tried, but her captor had not reeked of drink. And it had never ended. He had seemed perfectly content to lie beside her with only that hand at her throat, and the heat of him…did things to her. That body of his, that should have terrified her…didn't.

His arms had been so big around her. And she had always imagined men like rocks. Made of stone and so bewildering, so harsh. But he had been so warm. Hot to the touch, and the way he'd breathed beside her had made a treacherous languor steal through her, as if she'd spent the day out in the winter cold and had only now come in to sit by the fire.

Except he was the fire.

She could remember, with perfect clarity, when she had breathed out at last, and let it go.

Surrendering herself to him, by her own choice.

That fire in him had burned inside her ever since.

"Tell me what you want tonight," he bade her, in that low, deep rumble that she could feel in all the places he touched her. Her bottom, bright with his marks. The entirety of her middle, tied up so tightly in his ropes. And that hand, so hard she could feel her own pulse beat back at her. "Your murderous friend sleeps near. You know what will happen if she attempts to intervene. So tell me. What do you want, little slave?"

Eithne hardly knew how to answer him. She was lost somewhere in the shock of her realizations, but also focused intently on the promise in his gaze.

And there was no use trying to game this. Trying to decide what he wanted, or what was the best sort of answer, because in the end, it didn't matter. He would do what he would. She would hate it as it was happening and then dream of it later.

And then, so soon after, want more.

Always more. Always he was that hunger within her, keeping that hollow space ever open and that flame forever dancing.

There was a part of her that wanted to lie. That wanted to say that she wished for slumber, but she didn't dare. And not only because she thought he would laugh at that, and then do his worst. But because she *wanted* him to do his worst, and it felt as if, were she to lie about that, it would break something inside her.

She could not understand it, but there seemed to her no getting around it.

"I want," she said, the words somehow making her shake even worse. "I want what was promised."

She could see the gleam of approval in his gaze and that was nearly enough, as she squirmed where she knelt, to make her shatter.

"And what was promised, little slave? What is it you need as much as I do?"

Eithne felt that great sigh move through her then. She felt herself shudder, then release, surrendering.

Surrendering completely, her gaze locked to his. As if he held her there, too.

"I need your hands to remind me who we are," she whispered, as if these were words to a prayer she had known all her life. As if she were but reciting. "And the staff to remind me what was lost." But that was wrong. She shook her head, as much as she could in his grasp. "What I took, Master. To remind me what I took."

And she couldn't help the notion, then, that everything changed in that moment. That his gods tilted the earth beneath them and everything around them spun off into nothingness.

No kings to please. No wars to fight.

There was only this bright fire between them.

There was only the way she loved him and the surrender that, somehow, made her feel stronger.

There was only Ulfric and that slow, knowing smile that moved over his face and carved out a new hunger deep within her. There was only the way his hand tightened around her neck, just enough to make her breath catch in the way she liked it best.

And then, there in that tent with the rain above and Osthryth too close by, he taught her exactly how inventive he could be.

Without ever making a sound.

Chapter Thirteen

The last time Ulfric had returned to Dublin, it had been in a warship as a part of Ragnall's army, arriving to fight at Sitric's side to win back what had been taken from them long since.

This was different. This time they landed in a city already friendly. There was no need to come in, ready for battle, when those who thronged the docks to greet the ship were not foes.

This day, Ulfric disembarked amongst allies. Then he walked through a busy city, navigating his way through merchants hawking their wares, heavier ships with cargo from Norway, Denmark, the land of the Rus, the Arab lands, and more. There were so many languages spoken that the mess of them seemed to displace the air.

It felt like home.

And for once he was not required to fight his way into it.

Something about that thought made him grip Eithne's

neck more securely as they walked in their usual way, with her before him. He angled a look down at her, trying to divine her response in the way she held herself.

As if she were fragile yet trying her best not to appear so.

He had made the old woman walk ahead of them, lest he find a dagger in his back. For she was still disturbing, no matter that she was dressed as a grandmother now instead of a ghoul. They had found a village on the Mersey where Ulfric had parted with some silver to clothe the hag—for it would do him no honor to bring a ragged witch to Sitric's court, and well did he know it.

Osthryth had not been particularly grateful.

But Eithne had gazed at him as if he had draped fine jewels around her neck, and he did not care to ask himself why it was that a slave's delight should please him so. He suspected he already knew that answer and liked it little.

She had woken early this day, out there on the water. Ulfric rarely slept much at sea, and had been with the ship's captain, talking of subjects great and small as they cut through the Irish Sea. It was an easy sail from the mouth of the Mersey. The rest of the passengers had been asleep, huddled beneath their cloaks on the open deck. Ulfric had seen the moment Eithne woke. How she jolted, then looked around wildly, and it pleased him. For he knew she was looking for the ropes that normally tied her to his bed. A moment later, she pushed herself up on one arm, and though her eyes were still clouded with sleep, her gaze had come quick to his.

And he had stopped hearing what the man beside him was saying, for all he could hear was Eithne's voice in his head, sobbing out his name. A particular song he had not heard sung in too long now. For the old woman's presence was an inhibition. Not for Ulfric, but for Eithne, who remained certain that any moment her friend would hear them, cry rape, and come for Ulfric's throat.

He understood that what upset her was not the laughable possibility that the old woman might succeed in slitting his throat, but what he would do to her if she tried. Another thing that should not have concerned him, as what did it matter what a slave felt?

Yet he suspected he knew the answer to that, too.

Still, Ulfric had found a return to the silence that had once marked their encounters almost unbearably pleasurable. It made every touch, every reaction, sweeter, somehow. It had been both reminder and challenge, and his cock liked it so well he had to order himself to stand down as he walked.

As if she could sense the direction of his thoughts, the crone herself looked back over her shoulder then, her wizened old eyes meeting his boldly.

And Ulfric thought, not for the first time, that Osthryth were in no way confused about what happened between him and Eithne in the privacy of their tent. Not in the slightest.

But he dismissed her, returning his attention to the

streets they walked through, and the woman whose neck beneath his hand hinted at the turmoil she must feel within. It was only the faintest tremor that moved in her, but he knew her body too well. He knew that if he could feel her reaction there, there were far deeper ones she was fighting to conceal.

"Is it as you remember it?" he asked her, his gaze scanning the throngs of people around them, forever looking for threats. And for friends and foes alike, for there was no telling where either might lurk. "Or has the city changed past recognition?"

To his eye, it was little changed. Busier, perhaps. But then, he had helped burn down the Dublin she had known.

"I think it is I who have changed," Eithne said quietly. When he looked down, she was gazing around as if she was searching for the same threats he did.

"Nothing stays the same," said the old woman. "And those who wish otherwise find out their folly to their peril. For no summer has ever passed that does not turn to fall. And all things must die when winter comes. That is the way of it."

Eithne was nodding, a gentle rhythm against his palm. "The plants may return in spring," she said. "But they are never the same."

"We have been gone near on four years now," Ulfric said.

"It is a long time indeed," Eithne agreed, and he thought she sounded fragile then. He could not like it.

"Who can say who has lived this long? I am sure many I knew died in that battle. And many more since. It is possible there is no one left here who remembers me."

Yet she did not say that as if she believed it. For she remained too stiff. And her eyes were narrow now as she continued to look sharply into the shadows they passed. As if she expected to find something—or someone—she recognized in their depths.

But they were fast approaching Sitric's hall, and Ulfric had greater worries than what ghosts his woman might find here.

Your slave, he corrected himself.

There were the usual greetings as they walked toward the entrance to the hall. For it was not possible for a man dressed like a warrior as he was, and built like one who won the battles he faced, to simply walk into a castle to see a king. First he needed to prove who he was to Sitric's men.

"I come bearing a message from Ragnall," he declared as he faced off with the two who stood there, blocking his path. "And it is for no ear save Sitric's, for we are all kinsmen and Ragnall trusts his words only to his blood."

"If I had a bit of silver for every man who did attempt to gain entrance to this hall, claiming to share blood with these great kings, a wealthy man I would be indeed," said one of the men, eyeing Ulfric with distaste.

But the other laughed, extending his hand in friendship. "I know this man," he told his compatriot. "For he and I did fight side by side on the Isle of Man, carrying Ragnall's banner. This is no other than Ulfric, brother to Thorbrand, both of them sons of Birger the Bloody, who did hold the line here in Dublin for a day and a night before succumbing. Great were the songs we sang to remember him." He clasped Ulfric's hand. "It is I, Njal, who am sometimes called mighty. And I have heard songs sung of your deeds, my friend. Many are the tales of brave Ulfric the Grim, whose bow never misses and whose blade swings strong."

"Such songs pale in comparison to those I have heard," replied Ulfric in kind. "Of the courageous Njal the Mighty, son of Toki, who the gods themselves favor. Whose enemies but whisper his name, lest they summon him. For sharp is his blade, deadly his club, and none who stand against him prosper."

Njal let out another laugh, this one of clear welcome, and so did Ulfric make his way into Sitric's hall, where there were a great many familiar faces—or men whose deeds were known to him. It was in this way he was led to one of the long tables. He was seated, his women beside him, and they were all given bowls of last night's rich stew, fresh bread, and ale to quench their thirst.

Osthryth looked as if she would rather throw her bowl at someone's head, but she wisely chose to eat instead. Beside him, her leg pressed tight to his, Eithne ate well. Yet she still spent too much time for his liking casting her gaze about, still looking for her ghosts in the shadows.

But then the King entered the hall, and Ulfric could worry no more about his slave.

For Sitric was an ally. He and Ragnall were not only kin, but great friends.

But he was not Ulfric's king. He was not the man Ulfric had vowed to honor, pledging his life.

And it required a set of skills that had always better suited his brother, to Ulfric's mind. The delicate balance of respect and fealty, without appearing neither too grandiose, nor too obsequious.

These were the courtly games he despised. Far better, to his mind, the straightforward swing of a blade. The simple honesty of battle. For sure enough, there were strategies and campaigns, and no shortage of machinations on battlefield, but there all depended on strength and skill.

In Ragnall's court, particularly when his generals were dispatched to hold the line elsewhere, Ulfric knew well the currents and what moved beneath them. But in Sitric's court, he was a stranger. He risked drowning at any moment if he wasn't careful.

"I have waited for word from my kinsman," said Sitric as he threw himself into his chair at the head of the table. "But your name is known to me, too. Ulfric, son of Birger the Bloody." He tapped his cheek, then he drew a line across it. "I have heard it said that despite your feats on many a battlefield from the Isle of Man to Waterford, here in Dublin and all across Northumbria, it was a slave girl who cut you down."

A cold fury moved inside Ulfric's chest then, but he was not foolish enough to indulge it. Some men shared out their slave girls. It was not an outrage that another man might make reference to her, especially not when he wore that scar. And yet he longed to swing his fist, at the very least.

He did not. He inclined his head to the King instead, for he valued his life and so too Ragnall's standing here.

"Better a blade than a bended knee," he said. He met Sitric's gaze, finding him as hardy as he recalled him, with only the faintest touch of silver at his temples. "And it is a wise master who does not react but waits. So that reparations are the sweeter."

For a moment, Sitric only studied him. Then he let out a deep laugh. "She must be a comely slave indeed for man to give her such freedom with his blade."

He looked at Eithne beside Ulfric, more intently than Ulfric liked. Ulfric smiled as if he did not have the sudden, mad urge to introduce the side of his sword into this conversation, lest the King think it acceptable that he gaze upon Eithne in that carnal manner.

Yet how else did he imagine men would look at her? She was but a slave. And he kept her too well, and too pretty—leaving no one in any doubt what her true duties must entail. Beside him, Eithne kept her gaze demurely lowered as if she knew not that she was the topic of conversation, but Ulfric could see the telltale smudge of red at the tips of her ears and knew better.

It sat uneasily on him that he could not protect her

from this. She was a slave and slaves had no rights. He could not claim them on her behalf. Most men did not dare risk Ulfric's displeasure, but Sitric was not most men. He was a king, his power greater even than Ragnall's.

Ulfric had no choice but to act as if the King's words amused him. "What good can a blade be if a man does not risk its sting?"

"Well do you speak," Sitric said with a grunt. He nodded, his gaze much like Ragnall's then, canny and intense. "I see why my kinsman sent you to represent him here. You do him credit."

Ulfric did not pretend he was unaware of the great compliment the King paid him. "It is my honor and privilege to speak on behalf of Ragnall, as best I am able."

Sitric rose then, beckoning that Ulfric should follow him. He could do not but obey, though as he rose, he glanced at Eithne beside him. And he thought that for all she made a pretty picture as a demure slave, head meekly lowered, the truth was there in her green eyes. He saw the flicker of flame dance there, alight with all the things she dared not say here in Sitric's court.

He wanted to haul her up by the ropes she wore and secure her to the wall. To the bench. To the table itself.

But he knew that if he did so, it would do naught but make him appear weak. He might not have cared about that overmuch, for he could always challenge such notions in battle, but if he looked weak here then so too did Ragnall. And that he could not abide.

He was forced to admit, as he turned from her and followed Sitric out of the great hall, that he did not know what Eithne would do. She might take this as an opportunity to run again. For all he knew, her brother was one of the men in the hall, waiting only for her master to quit the room so he could aid in her escape.

But he remembered what she had said to Ragnall back in Jorvik. That all slaves would take their chances with an escape if they could. For who wished to be a slave? No enemy would let Ulfric live if they defeated him in battle, he knew this well, but still. He could not say that he would care overmuch for the state of slavery. He would like it still less if his own brother sold him into it.

But his true objection to slavery, he accepted as he was forced to walk out of the room and leave Eithne behind—only hoping that she would be there when he returned—was that because of it, he could never know if his woman stayed with him by choice. For she had no choices.

It was being back in Dublin that made him think these things. For perhaps he had relied too much on the fact that most of their time together was spent in foreign lands, where she had no friends. Where there were none who might stand for her, and he was not required to think of such matters.

He pressed the heel of his palm to his chest as Sitric led him into a smaller room off the hall. The King here sank into a grand chair, and then waved a hand.

Bidding Ulfric give him the message he had traveled all this way to deliver.

Ragnall had seen to it that Ulfric memorized every word, for it was a long message that could have been trusted only to so loyal a man as Ulfric. For there were messengers aplenty, and many who could carry the usual requests, needs, or talk of movements. But Ragnall was worried about Edward amassing men on the Mercian border. He was worried about the Danes, who were increasingly more Christian and more likely to support the Christian King of Wessex than Ragnall, or in turn, Sitric. For it was one thing to fight for land. This clash of gods was different. It was more dangerous. For men might yield territory when it was naught but their own self-interest on the line. But when they fought for the glory of their gods, they could not yield. They would not.

Two of Ragnall's generals were even now in position, and ready to do more than simply maintain their defenses against the inevitable Wessex incursion, but Ragnall had requested Sitric's counsel. For Edward was relentless. And while Ragnall had no love for the selfish Christian God, he did wonder whether seeming to embrace him might lead, at the very least, to some kind of peace in Northumbria.

All of this did Ulfric dutifully repeat, just as Ragnall had said it.

When he was done, Sitric sat back in his chair and rubbed his hand over his beard. His expression gave nothing away. "Does he expect you to bring him a reply?"

"If it please you to reply, then yes. He would have me relay your words to him."

"I will have to think on it," Sitric replied, after a moment. "The world is changing. Kingdoms grow ever larger on these islands. Edward would rule us all if he were but able."

Ulfric felt the corner of his mouth lift. "Would you not do the same?"

For a moment, he thought he'd gone too far. But in the next breath, Sitric threw back his head and roared with laughter. "Therein lies the trouble," he said, still laughing as he spoke. "For there are too few kingdoms and too many kings to rule them. What will become of us all?"

Then he stood and clapped Ulfric on the back. "I will have your answer, but there are those I must consult."

"I understand," Ulfric said, inclining his head. For he knew well that great men always liked to ponder their every move far in advance.

"Treat Dublin as your home as it once was, and my hall as a place to lie your head," Sitric continued, as he headed back for the great room where his men waited for him. "For I would honor my kinsman Ragnall with my hospitality, and you, Ulfric, whose deeds have honored our blood for years, deserve no less."

"You do me a great honor, sire," Ulfric said, and meant it. "Any deeds of mine only pale next to the glory of yours, for do you not stand in the city you took back from the Irish Kings yourself?"

"I remember well who else stood at my side," Sitric replied. "Tonight, we will sing of it."

Ulfric knew well he should have felt Sitric's praise like warm mead flowing through his veins. Yet all he cared about was looking immediately for Eithne—and only allowing himself a full breath when he saw her sitting right where he had left her.

His heart knocked at his ribs like a battering ram.

He was sure it must have showed on his face.

Still, he promised Sitric to return for the evening meal, and made some claim that he had other business that needed his attention in the city, which was not a lie. It was only that his business involved his slave.

And his need to be inside her, now.

He did not think that the hospitality on offer in Sitric's hall would grant them the privacy he craved after days on the road with Osthryth as witness, followed by a journey across the sea in an open boat. But this was Dublin. Like Jorvik, anything could be found here for a price.

Especially in summer, when staying warm and dry was not a priority.

"Where is the crone?" he asked gruffly as Eithne stood, breathing in full only when he wrapped his palm around her nape. And could feel her, right where she belonged.

"She bade me remind you that she is neither your

slave nor your servant," Eithne told him with mischief in her gaze, at odds with her diffident voice. "And as such, has gone to look for healer women, that she might learn something new to her. She did not say it would be poison. But she also did not swear it would not."

Ulfric would have laughed at that, had they been alone. But here in this hall there were too many eyes watching him. His conduct at all times must shine glory upon Ragnall. He dared not laugh overmuch with the slave girl too many already knew too much about.

But he and Eithne knew each other too well. And words had never been their primary form of communication. As easily as he could see the mischief in her gaze did she read the laughter in his, and he knew then that she understood the stakes today. For all she did was press her lips together to keep them from curving, then directed her gaze to the floor.

It took some while to leave the hall, for news of who Ulfric was and Sitric's warm reception of him had spread. So men gathered around, speaking of battles they had fought together, deeds they had heard told in song. And then, the niceties observed, asking for news of their kin and their comrades in Northumbria.

And Ulfric, though never much for talking when deeds would do, knew well the importance of the news he could bring. For as small as the world might feel these days, as Sitric had said—they were all isolated come winter. When the seas raged and storms held these islands in their grip, only fools dared tempt the gods by taking to the waves. Men who risked such journeys rarely returned. So he gave what news he could. He spoke to each man in turn and when he was done would have strode immediately from the hall had not Eithne ever so slightly nodded her head in the direction of the women he would not have noticed. The women who waited quietly and meekly to the side, doing nothing to attract his attention.

"Do you seek news?" he asked them and felt a kind of shame in him as he did so that he had not thought to ask on his own. When he had spent over a year asking for such news himself, and had been in no way fussy about who brought it.

He remembered, suddenly, all the things Eithne had said about men and women in these weeks since he'd had her back. How she had repeatedly drawn his attention not only to her slavery, but the fate of women overall. Maybe because he had spent all this time so focused on one woman, he found that he was better able to think differently about the rest.

Not as potential bedmates, for most women would not care for the sport he liked best. Not as helpful cup bearers, quiet servants, or other men's wives. But as people, just like Eithne, with lives perhaps as complicated as hers. People lost, family and friends torn away, and some sent off to far-flung bits of earth with no hope of return.

Maybe if his mother had lived past the worst of his

callow youth. Maybe if he had sisters of his own. Maybe it would not have taken him this long—

But this was no time to think such revolutionary thoughts. Instead, Ulfric took his time with the women who gathered around him. He answered their questions about kinfolk they had not seen in years, not since many of them had left with Ragnall, and gave what news he could, aware all the while of the woman who stood beside him and the heat between them that he still could not quite believe no one else felt.

"Thank you for that kindness," Eithne said with unusual softness—vulnerability, he thought—when they finally walked out of the hall. "Those are not all free women. They had no expectation that you would condescend to notice them, much less speak to them of those they have lost."

Inside him, Ulfric felt a new storm brewing. And as ever, he did not wish to face it head-on. He wanted only to get rid of it.

And he knew of one way in particular that he might manage it. The way he always managed it. A cock cared little for the feelings of any but itself.

The crowded bustle of Dublin surrounded them, and Ulfric could take no more of this. He saw an alley between two buildings and maneuvered her into it, backing her up against a wall, his blood high and hot. His cock hard enough that he might yet use it as a blade.

"Eithne," he said, his voice low, rough. As if he was

not himself. As if he might never be himself again.

"Eithne, I—"

But then he felt, impossibly, the prick of a real blade—digging in just enough to break the skin.

Just enough to announce itself and enrage him.

For he could identify it at once. It was steel, implacable and deadly.

And it was there at his back.

Chapter Fourteen

Above her, his mouth nearly touching hers, Ulfric froze.

At first, Eithne didn't understand. She stared up at him as his face changed. As her Ulfric disappeared, and in its place came the stern, fearsome warrior.

She knew this face well. Many times had she seen it as they'd marched across Northumbria. Many times before he went into battle. And again when he returned, bleak murder in his gaze, with bruises and scrapes and deeper wounds she would patch up for him before the fire, slowly bringing him back to her.

Though it had taken some time to admit to herself that she thought of it thus, for she had wanted—badly—to detest him. She had tried her best.

Ulfric pushed away from her and then turned, so that she had the protection of his back. A back that had a bleeding wound in its center, though he did not seem to feel it, and she had to look around his massive arm to see—

No.

It was not possible.

She could not take in what she saw before her. She could not make sense of it.

Her head spun and if Ulfric had not been there before her, a mountain of a man who could have held the whole of Dublin on his shoulders, or so it seemed to her, then surely she would have collapsed into the dirt at their feet.

She nearly did anyway.

"I knew it was you," came the querulous voice of the man who stood before them, brandishing a wicked-looking dagger. The tip of it was dark, and Eithne realized he must have used it. That he must have made that wound even now bleeding on Ulfric's back.

There was something inside her then, loud and long. Like a howl.

Though if he was hurt, if he even felt it, he gave no sign. He stood tall as ever, and from him came wave after wave of fury and power.

"I knew it was you, you bloody great bastard," said the man, and Eithne had to force the haze of her own reaction away from her eyes, so she might look at him again. So she might make certain that she saw what she thought she did. "Marching her about like a common whore."

"Stick that dagger in me again," Ulfric invited him, his voice enough to strike terror into all he faced. It made her wince and it was not directed at her. "But not in the back, like a coward. See how you fare."

The man before him only curled his lip. And Eithne was having trouble believing what her eyes yet told her.

For she knew this man, though these near four years had not been kind to him. When she had last seen him, he had been overweening, filled with pride and ale and in possession of all his hair. Today there was no hint of that man, who had always fancied himself one battle away from greatness.

If there had been a battle, he had not won it. No songs would be sung of his deeds. He looked sickly. He reeked. His beard and hair were matted and his clothing stiff and dirty, and though Eithne knew that she had been ruined by what the priests called the Northman vanity—the need to bathe themselves so often, the desire to attire themselves too brightly, the abiding interest in keeping their appearance pleasing—this was not simply a difference in cultures. This looked like a hard, long fall from even the standards she had been raised with, where cleaning and grooming oneself were expected, if not as often as the Northmen required it.

Eithne told herself that if she had any Christian charity within her, as the priests had taught, she ought to feel it now.

But instead, all she felt was a deep and terrible fury.

"Do you call me a whore?" she demanded from behind Ulfric's arm. She shoved at it, but he did not move so much as a hair. "Do you dare, Feargal?"

For this was her brother, this dirty, diminished man. This was the creature who had held such power over her life that he had sold her to a slave trader so he might have some silver to bargain with once the Northmen had taken the city. And yet he had let the man bargain him down to only a few pieces of silver.

A pittance. That was what he had sold her for.

And look what had become of him.

"Not that you look the worse for it," Feargal sneered at her. "Tarted up like a Northman's *frilla*."

The Northman word for concubine sounded like a filthy insult in Feargal's mouth.

"That is what I am," Eithne said, her words coming from her mouth like stones while there were only daggers in her heart, her eyes. "Did you think you sold me so I might become a Northman's queen instead?"

"Be very careful, friend," Ulfric said to Feargal before he could answer his sister, in that particular rumble of a low voice that set off small fires all the way down Eithne's spine. For she knew very well the danger he posed. And the damage he could do—only think what he did to her for his pleasure. "For this Northman is possessive of his property and takes it ill when others do not respect it."

Eithne was almost touched by that defense, truly, but she was too focused on her brother.

"What think you our parents would say if they knew?" she demanded, and pushed against the unyielding wall that was Ulfric, trying to get around him. She failed. So all she could do was point her finger at the man who had betrayed her. The man who had ruined her. She knew, deep inside, that there was likely something wrong with her that the man she pointed to was not he who now owned her. But instead the brother who should have saved her from this fate. "Do you imagine our father would thank God for a son such as you? To bring such dishonor onto our family name?"

"Says a dirty whore," Feargal threw back at her. "I thought to rescue you, but you look far too well-fed to need any rescuing. Do you earn it on your back? Have you spent these long years rutting with him and all his savage friends? Keeping your belly warm and his cock hard while the family you left behind yet starves?"

There was a deadly sound, low and fierce, that it took her a moment to realize was Ulfric. Growling at Feargal in warning.

"Did I have a choice in where I was taken?" Eithne threw back at her brother, because she did not fear Ulfric. Not like this. She feared him far more when he smiled at her as if he pitied her, then made her beg for the exquisite pain and glory he would bestow upon her. "Or who took from me what they liked? If these things bothered you, Feargal, you should not have made me a slave. So that any who wished could do as they liked with me. Did you think they would not?" She let out a bitter laugh. "You need not answer. I know well you do not think of me at all."

Ulfric made another low noise, but she ignored him,

pushing against him again and yet again managing to move him but little.

"Did you enjoy what little silver you got for me?" she asked her brother. "It does not look as if you used it well. Let me guess. You sold your sister off into an uncertain fate and spent what little you made on carousing. And yet I am unsurprised to find that all these years later, you have convinced yourself that the fault is somehow mine."

"I couldn't believe it when I saw you walk by." Feargal was still waving that dagger in the general direction of Ulfric, who looked about as bothered by Feargal and the threat he represented as a mountain might. "As prim as you please. In a fine dress, not the rags of your station. Braids in your hair as if you could be a free woman. You look very little like a slave, sister. How well the state must suit you."

"That I have not already died a grim and horrible death is no thanks to you," Eithne seethed at him. "That my captor is no monster is no more than chance. A quirk of fate, and no more. You did not stick around the slave market to find out. You took your silver and you went, leaving me behind. Do not let us lie to each other now, brother. Let us not pretend that you have spared me a single thought or prayer in the years between. Let us not fool ourselves. You feel no sorrow for my welfare. You are only angry that despite the horror you chose for me, I have come through it better than you."

She could not have said where those words came

from. The girl he had sold might have thought such things, yet never would she have dared speak them aloud. She had prayed many times that Feargal's heart might change, and with it his terrible decisions, but that had been between her and God. She had never confronted him. It would never have occurred to her that she could, for like it or no, he was the head of their family.

But Eithne was not the girl he'd gotten rid of. She was the girl who had lived through his betrayal.

She was the meek, obedient girl who had found her place at the side of a terrifying Northman, and she was the one who had escaped him, too. Eithne was a woman who had lived by her wits in the woods, obedient and meek to no man. She was the slave who had lived through being caught again, too.

And she had even fallen in love with the last man alive who should have captured her heart, though he had captured all the rest of her.

She didn't know what it meant for her, to love her captor. It felt as much a ruin as a joy in her heart, though she could not deny it was that joy. And she were already ruined, surely. Perhaps it could not matter.

Eithne told herself it did not, but something in her shook at that lie.

For loving Ulfric was no small thing, no small joy.

Worse, she was certain that soon enough, he would know it. And then she would not only be his slave—she would have handed him the means to ensure that she never, ever ran from him again. A chain she could never break.

She could not think of these things now. Not here, and not while her brother watched.

Not while he held a knife on her and the man she loved.

She was no longer the girl he knew.

She was not, and had not been for some while, the girl he'd cast aside so callously, so selfishly, and thought so little of since.

Feargal had no idea who he was dealing with this day.

"Why should you wear fine wool while your brother wears rags?" he was demanding. "Have you forgotten your place?"

"And what place is that, please?" Eithne queried, with far more fury in her voice than she would ever dare show Ulfric, for she knew too well how he would take it. "I am but a lowly slave. You are not my master. What I do is of no concern to you."

"But it is of great concern to me," Ulfric growled then, glaring down at Feargal. "And if you do not put away that dagger, I cannot vouch for where it will end up."

"You swaggering Northmen are all the same," Feargal snarled at him. "Like packs of dogs, swarming everywhere, lifting your legs and claiming what is not yours."

"Because you Irishmen are covered in glory," Ulfric

replied, and though Eithne could hear a note of amusement in his voice, that did not change the way he stood, immovable—and too capable of keeping her in place without even glancing her way. Without showing the faintest shred of disquiet. As if he were wounded and had weapons pointed at him all the time—

She almost laughed, then. Because, of course, he did.

Feargal ignored the giant of a man before him, and surely nothing could have convinced her more that he was utterly mad. The older brother she had admired as a child, then found a grave disappointment when it was her lot to care for him, had become…this. A lost man, reduced to little more than a beggar in the street, who somehow failed to recognize the grave threat before him.

He clearly cared not at all about his sister, his only remaining kin. She had known this, of course, but time had dulled the truth of it. Time had made her question her memories.

All these years, she'd nursed her fury at what he'd done. But that had only been a mask for the betrayal. Many nights she had lain awake, imagining some kind of revenge, but it had never occurred to her that fate would throw him in her path like this.

As if fate had taken revenge on him already.

And she supposed she could not be too surprised at his reaction now. In comparison to Feargal, who her parents had once believed would bring glory to their name, she had prospered. As a slave to their greatest enemy. No wonder he could not accept it.

For herself, she found that beneath the fury, beyond the betrayal, there was the part of her that had so dearly loved Fainche. There was the girl who had adored her mother and deeply admired her father. She had loved her brother, too.

And this part of her grieved. For the brother Feargal had never been. For the man he would never become.

For the brother she should have had, who would have allowed her to be sold as she had been only over his dead body.

But her grief was hers. She did not need to share it with the creature before her now. Indeed, she felt free of it, at long last.

More, she knew well that it was Ulfric who had taught her how to find wings in the most unlikely places. Who had painstakingly showed her how to fly, so that no matter how much this hurt, she knew she would survive it.

And more than that, thrive.

"You look well enough," Feargal was saying in that accusing way of his. "I know many men who might have married you, and even now, though you have the stink of Northmen about you, they would pay well for a turn between your thighs. Only think what you must have learned in the furs of a brute like this."

Ulfric laughed then, loud. Long. He laughed, and he did not sound like the Ulfric she knew at all. Every hair on her body seemed to stand straight up. She had the urge to drop to her knees, to bow her head low, to do whatever must be done to weather what came next.

For she had seen Ulfric before battles. And again after them. She lived with him and took part in his favorite kind of struggle with him.

But never had she seen him in the middle of a real fight, ready to take down his enemy by any means.

For that laugh was the laugh of a mighty Northman warrior whose deeds she had heard described in shining detail only today, again and again in the King's hall. Ulfric the Grim, who had spent a lifetime learning to take down his enemies, one by one.

Feargal did not heed the warning. "I should have done this with you years ago. I could have fine linens. A warm fire. A roof above my head, where no drafts dare penetrate. I thought the shame of it would be too much."

Eithne made a noise, despite herself. Whether shock or horror, she could not have said. It was all the same now. "I'm delighted to know you thought of it, even so. What an honorable man you are, brother. How proud our ancestors must be."

"But what can shame matter?" Feargal was saying, ranting now, so that his face grew red, his bloodshot eyes bulged, and spittle flew. "You were not here these last years, sister. You know not what it has been like, to live under the yoke of these savages."

"Do I not?" Eithne retorted, feeling her temper

charge through her. "I, who live as a slave to a Northman master? You think *I* do not know a yoke?"

She glanced up at Ulfric as she said it and thought she saw some odd hint of approval in his gaze, where surely there should have been none.

"Whoring agrees with you, sister," Feargal sneered at her, his gaze an insult. "Better I should profit on it than this animal."

And everything then seemed to happen both too fast and too slow.

Feargal lunged forward with a knife, but Ulfric only laughed. And waited an eternity, it seemed to her, before batting the knife from Feargal's hand with a blow hard enough it sent her brother to the ground.

Then Ulfric stepped forward, opening his hands wide. "Is that all you have?" he demanded. "Tell me more of what is you will do with my woman. I dare you."

Feargal, crouched down in the alley where Ulfric's blow had tossed him, rose. This time, he held a small axe he must have held beneath his cloak.

He lunged toward Ulfric. Ulfric laughed again, moving to take the axe—

But Eithne was behind him still. And she could see that Ulfric was focused on the axe, and did not see a new dagger in Feargal's other hand—

But she did.

And it all seemed to race through her then. Every memory, every sensation. Everything. Like her life was a song sung to her then, no deta.. ...no moment forgotten.

Long-ago days in her parents' small, resp.. home, gathered around the fire beneath the tha.. roof. Feargal's laughter, back then. The way he ... gazed upon their father, with love and a boy's worship, as if he intended to be the same kind of man someday. Honest, just. Good.

And she felt, too, that grief.

Eithne wondered what might have become of them if their family had lived. If the Northmen had not come. If they had lived out their lives in peace, though she knew there was precious little of that to go around.

She would always wonder who her brother might have been if they had not lost so much. If it had not broken something in him the way it had in her, too. Though she had not acted on it as he did.

But here, now, she could not mourn the man he was not. She could only handle the man he was.

A scheming, venal man who would whore out a sister he had already sold into slavery, if he could. A man who thought he was owed her degradation and suffering, should it profit him.

A man who would kill Ulfric, and though she could likely survive the rest, *that* she could not have.

For no matter how many other complications it was braided with, or how it felt inside her, she loved him. No matter what it made her.

She thought that in his way, he loved her, too.

And ... world like theirs? Even Ulfric, so full of truly ... courage, must answer to a king. More than strength they would not be here today.

... of this rushed through her, and she did not stop think.

Eithne threw herself forward, reaching for that dagger she'd taken from Ulfric's belt before. Only this time, he wore the belt as she went for it. Once again did she pull it out and feel the weight of it in her hard, smooth and heavy.

And as Feargal's hand slashed through the air, Ulfric turned, but it did not matter.

For she was the one to throw herself into the space between, hold up that dagger, and put it to her brother's throat.

"You would not dare to harm your own brother," Feargal snarled at her. "I am the only family you have." And then he called her a name so vile in the old language it made her pale.

"I have no family," Eithne whispered back.

And when he lunged forward, she did not drop her hand.

She called his bluff.

Ulfric moved fast. He pulled her away, cradling her head so that she could not look at the thing she'd done.

She heard another noise, a terrible one. And then all was quiet.

Ulfric seemed to take a very long time to look down at her.

His dark eyes were troubled. And she, who knew every expression that ever crossed his face, had never seen that particular light in his gaze before.

"You would kill your own brother?" he asked, echoing Feargal's query.

Though the way he asked it was…different, somehow.

And all those things that still raced around inside of her seemed overlarge, unwieldy. She could feel them begin to leak out of her eyes, but she did nothing to dash them away.

"If anyone will kill you, Ulfric, it will be me," she managed to say, though her throat was scratchy.

For what else could she say? She thought he would laugh. She thought, at the very least, she would see the glimmer of that dark amusement in his gaze, and all would be as it should.

But instead, he looked almost…dazed. As if he had taken a blow to the head, though she did not think it so.

"You thought you needed to save me," he said, and it took her a jarring thud inside her chest to understand that note she heard in his voice was wonder. "You picked up that dagger and fought, little slave. Your own brother. For me."

She could say nothing. She felt a rattling inside her, as if her very bones demanded that she defend her decision, but she had naught to say.

Eithne knew only that she felt as if she stood, again, at the edge of a very high cliff.

But then, she already knew that she would fly. It was only a question of when. And how far.

Ulfric reached out his hand, the way he often did, but only when he had caused her some of that wondrous pain.

His hand found her cheek, his thumb moved over her lips.

And something in her shook.

"I would give you anything," he told her, his voice so deep it seemed to come from some new place beside him. "For I owe you a debt. You acted to save my life. You valued it above your brother's. I could shower you in the finest furs. I could drape you in jewels from ports all over the world. But I know well, little slave, that there is only one thing you truly want."

"Ulfric…" she whispered, his name a touch of fire in her mouth.

"I have always thought myself a simple man," he told her then. And there was a bleakness in his gaze. An urgency she could not understand in his voice. His hand at her cheek almost seemed to shake, but he dropped it. And she knew she must be mistaken, for this was Ulfric, and nothing shook him. Nothing ever could. "But I realize now that what I am is selfish. Long have I wanted you to come to me because you wish it. To play these games because you need them as I do. I think you do. I think that you and I, Eithne, are but two halves of the same whole. I believe this, yet I tie you up—and not only for my own pleasure, but to guard against your escape. Today, I did not wish to leave you alone in that hall, for fear you would run from me once more."

"It didn't even occur to me," she whispered. It had not. She had sat where she was, the picture of obedience. So much so that Osthryth had been disgusted. That was why she'd gone to seek healer women in the market. *Perhaps I might find an herb to break this spell he has you under,* she had said.

Because Eithne had not been sitting there like that out of fear. She'd been sitting like that because she had wanted her behavior to reflect well on Ulfric.

One more truth she little wished to face.

"I cannot change this world we live in," Ulfric said. "I cannot change our fates. Only we can do that for ourselves by trying, every moment, to make the most of what we have. And I, who consider myself a brave man who fears nothing, cannot lie to myself about this any longer."

That shaking deep inside her turned to a kind of anguish. "Ulfric, I don't—"

"I can tell myself in a thousand ways that I can predict your every move. And that is so, but only because you are my slave. Because, as you have said to me on too many occasions to count, you have no choices." There was pain on his face, and she hated it. She *hated* it. Even his hand at her cheek was pain. But he did not pause. "And so this is the gift that I give to you, Eithne of Dublin and Northumbria. Your choice."

She couldn't have spoken then if her life had hung in the balance. Her heart beat too loud. Her bones ached. Eithne searched his face, not sure she hoped or disbelieved—

"You have earned your freedom, little slave," Ulfric told her, with great solemnity, though his dark eyes burned. "You are a free woman."

And she knew not what moved over his face then, only that it made a kind of sob burst free from her chest.

Joy, she told herself firmly, for what else could it be?

And on the other side of that narrow blade, grief.

Ulfric shifted his hand from her cheek to her neck, and caressed her there, in that place that longed for him to hold her. Then he led her out of the alley and onto the street, not using the nape of her neck to compel her to go where he wished, and she felt lost.

It only dimly occurred to her that he did this that she might not look back and see what had become of Feargal.

Because even now, he thought of her. And was this not the whole problem with this man? Her captor and owner? Was this not what had torn at her all along?

For he had never given her the opportunity to hate him as she should.

Not even back at the start, where trying to hate him was all she thought about.

Out in the busy street, he looked down at her again.

His hand not at her throat, but on her arm, and when he dropped it, she let out a small sound of distress.

And more, saw that same distress reflected in him.

As if it was as he said, and the two of them truly were one. One dark heart that only beat as it should together.

"Be well, Eithne," he told her, his voice gruff. Darker in that moment than she had ever heard it. "For I release you. You need only come to Sitric's hall tonight and I will tell them all. That I have freed you, and they must all treat you as they would any other free woman, with the rights and respect you deserve or they will answer to my sword. Even if it be Sitric himself."

Then he stepped back, and she had the notion he forced himself to do it. For a moment he did not move. And though she wanted to reach out, put her hands on him, *do* something—

She could not.

Ulfric inclined his head, though his eyes were fire.

Then he turned, and walked away, leaving her clinging to the side of a thatched hut in a city no longer hers, free at last.

He did not turn back. He did not stop. He walked until she could see him no more.

She took a breath. She took another, and the ropes that yet clung to her body dug deep, holding her as he had done.

As he never would again.

When she loved him as she did.

When he must love her, too, to call her the other half to make him whole.

When he had set her free, not because he wished to be done with her, but because he knew it was what she wanted above all things.

She was free, at long last, and she knew she should have been overcome with joy…but that was not what washed over her.

Because the thing she'd thought would never happen had happened, and she could not enjoy it as she had imagined she would all this time.

For now she could have the life she wanted, the life she deserved. The life that her brother had taken from her. She was no longer stranded in a foreign land. She was come home at last and Dublin was hers once more. She was sure she could find those who might know her family, if she wished. Or build a new life all her own. She could take up with Osthryth and dance as she pleased in the forests, no longer looking back over her shoulder.

She could do anything she liked. Anything she wanted, or near enough, for she was still a woman and men were ever men.

But it turned out that all she wanted was Ulfric, slave or free.

And so it was that Eithne's first act of freedom, so hard won after all these years, was to burst into tears.

Chapter Fifteen

That night Ulfric was given a place of honor at Sitric's table. His cup was filled first, and often. He knew well that he sat in Ragnall's stead, and so he drank for his King and honored his King's kin. He acquitted himself in a manner he knew could only be pleasing to Ragnall once he heard of it, for hear of it he would. Not only from Ulfric's own mouth, but from his many spies, too—some known to Ulfric and some not.

He should have been paying more attention to these weighty matters, he knew that well.

But all he could think of was Eithne.

His Eithne, who he had left behind. Who he had set free.

Already, everything in him roared at him to seek her out. To find her, now, and do whatever he must to bind her to him forever.

He did not know how he stayed at this table, the mead in his cup like ash to him.

All he could see was that scene in the alley. Eithne

could not have known that he would not have let her fool of a brother stick that knife into him. She had defended him as if he faced mortal danger.

He would have handsomely rewarded any man who had done the same.

Surely it meant even more that she was a mere woman, who could not have imagined she could cause too much harm. And more, a slave, whose love for her master could never be assumed.

The word *love* echoed inside him unpleasantly, as if it lodged in his bones.

"I keep looking to see a new scar upon your face," Sitric said from his place at the head of the table.

Ulfric tried to school his expression to stillness, but when the King laughed, he accepted it was likely he'd failed. "I have enough scars as it is," was all he said in reply.

"The last time your slave girl left you, she marked you on your way out." Sitric leaned back as he sat, looking merry and humble, lazy and unimposing. All of Ulfric's instincts told him to beware—for this king was none of those things. He only wished to let others think he might be. "And yet she lives on. Or so I have heard it told. Where is she now? Did you finally strike her down?"

Ulfric liked this man talking of Eithne so little it was tempting to do something to show it, but he hoped he was not so much of a fool. Especially when it was almost certain that Sitric was testing him. As kings loved to do, in his experience.

He set down his cup and prepared himself to play these games—

"He did something far worse than that, sire," came a voice he had not expected to hear again. Not here. Not now. He didn't believe it, yet when he looked up, she was there. His Eithne, standing before him, straight and tall in a way that told him at a glance that she yet wore the ropes he had tied around her. But her gaze was on Sitric. "He gave me my freedom."

Sitric propped up his chin on his fist, considering her. "Did he now?"

"It is true," she said, with remarkable calm and the sort of voice that reached every ear in the hall without seeming to try, Ulfric thought with more pride in her than she would likely wish to know he felt. "I stand before you a free woman, back at last in the place where I was born, raised, and sold."

"Yet with a different king upon the throne." Sitric's voice was a silken menace. A trap, and Ulfric could not warn her. "How does your freedom feel, if it not be Irish?"

But he had underestimated his Eithne.

"I am lucky," she said, and he saw that gleam in her green eyes that had always told him how clever she was, even when she did not speak. "For well do I already know the rules of life with a Northman."

Sitric found that entertaining enough. His laughter

was uproarious. Ulfric tore his gaze away from Eithne long enough to look around the hall. Others were laughing—more than not, indicating that she was finding favor here. And far beyond the tables of laughing men, he saw Osthryth sitting with the women.

For once the crone was not looking at him with murder in her eyes. He would not say the look she gave him was fond. But it was not violent and that was something.

He looked back to Eithne, who still stood there with her hands folded before her, her head not quite bowed, but certainly not lifted higher, either. The way any woman might stand before a king, and he, who had always found courtly intrigue tedious, could still recognize what she was doing here. First, proclaiming her freedom. Possibly to prove she had won it, here where Ulfric could gainsay her if he wished. And second, to make certain that all these men who knew her as a slave knew better now.

She was protecting herself and she was using Sitric to do it.

And even though everything within him yearned to stand up and roar out that he alone would stand as her protector, if the need arose, he did not.

He only waited.

And quickly found that he was no better at it than he had ever been.

Sitric turned his attention back to Eithne. "You amuse me," he told her. "A slave who dares leave her mark on her master. A free woman who presents herself to the King who burned down her city. Ask me for a favor, woman, and I tell you now, I will grant it."

Ulfric thought he knew exactly what favor the King wished to grant her, and he knew not what he would tell Ragnall about this night. For if Sitric thought he would put his hands on Eithne, Ulfric would kill him, their linked kingdoms be damned.

"Thank you, sire," Eithne was saying, and very prettily at that. "I have but one wish. For I am as new here as if Dublin was never my home. I have no friends here."

She did not look at Ulfric when she said this and still he knew that she was thinking of that alley, and the sound her brother's neck had made when Ulfric had concluded that he could not be allowed to live. For he would only come for Eithne again.

Ulfric would not allow it.

"Kin is everything," said Sitric, who would have claimed sheep were everything, too, if he'd imagined that would sweeten Eithne toward him, Ulfric had no doubt.

"I know not how I will live." Eithne lifted her head then. She looked at Ulfric but briefly, a flash of the deepest green, then at Sitric. "I find myself in need of a husband."

Ulfric did not realize he stood then, but there he was. He pushed back from the table and stood there on his own feet, his hand already on his sword.

He hardly recognized the King's laughter, so focused was he on the other men and the way they looked at Eithne now. One move and he would kill them all.

He did not realize he had shouted such a thing until he heard his own voice come back at him.

And perhaps, later, he would regret saying such a thing out loud in the hall of a king not his own.

But he could not regret it now. He meant it.

"I have a hall full of men," Sitric told Eithne, sounding merrier by the moment. "I'm sure there must be one to your liking here." He waved a hand. "You may pick any one you like."

Ulfric heard some noise to suggest that there were men putting themselves forth as candidates, risking certain death the moment he turned, but his eyes were only for Eithne.

His beautiful Eithne, who gleamed before him, as if to lead him from the dark.

For her, he would follow. Only for her.

"I have requirements," Eithne said, but she smiled, lest anyone think a woman late a slave dared make demands of a king. "I am a free woman now. But I have been a slave and found my treatment there far better than many women who have always been free. I have no doubt that every man in your hall is honorable."

"Else they would not enjoy my mead," Sitric murmured, a clear warning.

Eithne inclined her head. But she glanced over toward Osthryth and the other women. "I know that is so. Yet I know, too, that women know men in ways that other men cannot. And you have given me a choice, sire. So I would choose, as my husband, the only man I can trust to treat me well."

"Eithne," Ulfric gritted out, from somewhere deep inside of him.

Where there was nothing but her.

"But I am not a slaver," she said, and then, finally, turned to face him, her lovely face solemn. "So it must be your choice, too, Ulfric."

Ulfric would have said that he knew joy. That he had experienced it a thousand times in this life. For he knew the teachings, that every man must make his life matter, taking every moment and using it to meet his fate as best he could. He would have said that joy was no stranger.

But he had never felt anything like he felt now.

And he did not trust himself to speak. Indeed, he had said enough already.

Instead, in full view of Sitric and the rest of his men, he swept Eithne up and into his arms.

And then kissed her, full and deep, there where they could all see.

Let them sing about it throughout the ages.

Eithne melted beneath him and he lifted his head before he took the kiss too deep, meeting the King's gaze.

"I will marry her," he said. "And I will beat off any other man who tries with my own hands."

Sitric nodded as if this were his plan all along. Maybe it was, for there were few craftier.

"I will pay her dowry," the King declared, pounding his cup against the table in emphasis. "To her grandmother over there." He lifted his cup toward Osthryth, who did not bare her teeth in reply—a gift indeed. Then he turned his gaze to Ulfric. "And we will have a wedding, Ulfric. A story worthy of sharing with others, perhaps those to the west of us."

Ulfric understood what he was saying. Sitric would send him on to Ísland—

But he didn't care. Sitric could send him to Yggdrasil, the tree of life itself, to hold the nine worlds together with his own hands and he would not mind.

Not if Eithne was with him.

He waited for Sitric's nod, and at a wave of the King's hand he turned, carrying her away from this hall, and all these watching eyes. As he moved, he heard the songs, the laughter.

They could sing the hall down for all he cared.

Ulfric did not intend to notice.

He took her back into the room that he had been given, which were simple enough. More than adequate for what he had planned.

First, though, he kissed her. He kissed her and he kissed her. He set her down and then they stared at each other, both panting. Both out of breath.

But both here.

"I did not think you would return," he growled at her.

"I love you," she said, as if it was a curse. "I thought I did before. Now, I know it."

"And I you, little slave," he said, and watched her face change. All of that light. All of that wonder. All of it his now. "Now that you have chosen me, there can be no question."

And as he looked at her, he felt his mouth move into a smile he could neither stop nor control. He watched her wonder grow complicated. Then, best of all, he watched that delicate shiver.

"Remember," she said, as if was warning him. As if she dared. "Once I marry you, I can divorce you."

"But you won't."

It was not arrogance. Not with Eithne, who knew his darkness. Who had lived with him there. And had come back to him anyway.

She had left him once. She would not leave him again.

He knew it as surely as if he were the Fates themselves, and had planned it to be so.

"Ulfric," she whispered. "You set me free."

"I should have done it years ago," he replied, as if he confessed these things to her, as her people did their sins. "For there are any number of ways I might like to cause you pain, but like not that. Never again, my little slave."

She pinkened. "You will need to call me something else. I'm not a slave any longer. You made it so. And did you not hear your King?"

"But you will always be my slave, Eithne," Ulfric

said then, his voice rough. "Or did you forget who we are?"

And he watched as she flushed his favorite shade of red, then. He watched as her eyes heated and became glassy. He watched his woman as she wanted him in all the ways he wanted her.

This time, freely. Wholly.

"We will celebrate your freedom," he told her. "We will have a wedding. We will drink deep and dance. And someday you will give me sons, Eithne, who will grow up strong and brave and will tell stories wherever they go of the woman who raised them. Of her courage and her cleverness. Her loyalty and her love."

"Perhaps sooner than you think," she whispered, and only smiled a little when he lifted a brow. "When is the last time you gave me herbs to drink?"

He expected that to hit him badly, but instead, it sat in him like warmth. A new fire, but one he thought he would enjoy stoking higher.

Even now, his son could be in her belly.

But first there was this. A room in a hall in Dublin, where four years ago he had seen the truth of her as she stood in the slave market. Where today, he had seen a deeper truth when she had lunged forward and sunk a knife into her own brother on his behalf. She had not killed him. Ulfric had enjoyed that honor. Something he would tell her, so she need not grieve needlessly, if indeed she had such an urge for so worthless a man.

Yet not now.

"Eithne," he said, his mouth curving in the way she liked best. "Little slave. My only love. I think you know that you should be on your knees."

And all the storms he had carried in him all this time, that he would have said were dark, he found had been sunlight all along.

Because they burst through him, flooding him, as she smiled.

With nothing in that beautiful green gaze but love.

"I should," she agreed, making everything in him hum. "You will have to add that to the tally on the staff."

Then, as he watched, the woman who had long been his slave and would soon be his wife sank down to her knees before him.

Then bowed her head, just the way he liked it.

And this time, without there being the faintest shred of doubt between them that this had been entirely her choice all along.

Chapter Sixteen

They married that same summer, and Sitric was good to his word. He bestowed upon Osthryth a mighty dowry, making her a wealthy woman, a thought that made her cackle.

But he allowed them only a few days to revel in their marriage, then dispatched Ulfric to Ísland, where he was to gather more information. Then take it back to Dublin before returning at last to Jorvik.

Eithne thought that it did not much matter to her where she went. What mattered was that she go there with Ulfric. Even to these lands beyond imagining to the west.

Osthryth declared she loved Ísland and used the dowry Sitric had given her on Eithne's behalf to buy land. Ulfric met with his brother Thorbrand once more, and his wife, who called herself an ordinary Mercian, but spoke like a queen.

It was too near fall when they arrived, and the weather was not kind. The sea rose like a wall, and there was nothing for it but that they would spend the winter there—all worries about kings and their games left until spring.

Ulfric and his brother built them a small house near a tremendous waterfall and beach gone black. And every night, every day, in the splendid silence of this enchanted, isolated island, Eithne exalted in her choices. She chose to kneel before her husband. She chose, better still, the necklace he made her of hammered steel that sat around her neck like his hand might.

Come spring, when she was big with his child, she wore that necklace when he took his journey without her. Back to Dublin, then on to Jorvik, and he could not get home again quick enough to suit her.

For she brought his son into the world while he was off traveling it, and nursed the infant at her breast while she sang him the songs she'd heard in Sitric's hall. Tales of his father's many deeds and feats. Tales of Ulfric the Grim.

"But you will call him *faðir*," she whispered as she rocked him.

And freedom meant that the house they'd built was hers to run while her man was off doing his duty. Pride meant she did it well.

It was some years later, after Ragnall had died and Sitric had become King of Northumbria, that her husband came home to her and the babies they had made and told her he would travel no more. Though he had been gone near to a whole season this time, as he often was.

"But you are a warrior," she said calmly, though she wanted him here. She always wanted him here, but she knew who he was. And she would never stand in the way of what he needed. "Surely you must seek out what battles you can, wherever you may find them."

"There is only one battle that interests me any longer," he told her. And there was that smile she loved so much, crooking up the corner of his mouth. "It is the battle for your surrender, my little slave. And I feel that will sustain me in these winters dark and dreary. Kingdoms will have to rise and fall without me."

So indeed they did.

And come the long, cold nights they would find their way to the bedroom he had made them, with a door that shut tight, when the children were old enough to sleep without her. Ulfric no longer tied her to the posts, though they both liked her in the rope harness, and yet he always found new and creative ways to make her his.

Night after night. Season after season.

Each night they would leave their marks on each other, for that was the way of it. His on the outside, hers on the inside, making themselves into one.

And flying all the while.

Eithne had been a slave, and she had found him. Now she had him. And she was a free woman and a wife, a mother, and a friend to many, with his kinfolk who she now called hers—and eccentric, beloved Osthryth besides.

For they were braided all together now, love and

hope, joy and grief. His gods and hers and what magic lurked here on this island they called home.

And all of it was shot through with love.

But to make certain, Eithne chose it, as she had chosen all the things that truly mattered in her life.

Every day for the rest of their lives.

And the dream woke her in a rush every morning, his name on her lips.

Like a promise well-kept.

* * * * *

If you enjoyed this story, make sure to check out Caitlin Crews's dramatic Harlequin Historical debut

Kidnapped by the Viking